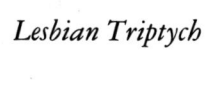

Lesbian Triptych

LESBIAN TRIPTYCH

Jovette Marchessault

translated by
Yvonne M. Klein

The
Women's
·Press·

CANADIAN CATALOGUING IN PUBLICATION DATA

Marchessault, Jovette, 1938-
[Tryptique lesbien. English]
Lesbian triptych

Translation of: Tryptique lesbien.
Bibliography: p. 97
Contents: Night cows – A lesbian chronicle
from medieval Quebec – The angel makers.
ISBN 0-88961-088-6

I. Title. II. Title: Tryptique lesbien. English.
III. Title: Night cows. IV. Title: A lesbian
chronicle from medieval Quebec. V. Title: The angel makers.

PS8576.A72T7913 1985 C848'.54 C85-098303-7
PQ3919.2.M37T7913 1985

Originally published in French as *Tryptique lesbien*
by Les éditions de la pleine lune
Copyright, Ottawa, 1980
ISBN 2-89024-003-7

This edition published with the assistance of Canada Council.

Copyright © 1985 by Women's Press

Cover illustration by Wendy Wortsman
Edited by Daphne Read
This book was produced by the collective effort
of the members of the Women's Press.
Printed and bound in Canada

First printing 1985
Second printing 1988

Published by The Women's Press
229 College Street No. 204
Toronto, Ontario M5T 1R4

CONTENTS

FLYING AWAY WITH LANGUAGE

Barbara Godard

JOVETTE MARCHESSAULT'S NAME has become known in feminist circles in English-speaking North America through Pol Pelletier's electric performance of "Night Cows," translated by Yvonne Klein. This piece appeared in print as part of *Tryptique lesbien,* a clearly political title which generated a backlash in Quebec that jeopardized Marchessault's growing literary reputation. Yet, since relatively little of the incredible creative production of Quebec feminists has been translated, the English reader may well wonder: who is Jovette Marchessault? How representative is her work of feminist writing in Quebec?

Jovette Marchessault is emerging as one of the major figures among contemporary Quebec feminist writers. The 1970s were marked by the dominance of the feminine on the literary scene. Women began to publish in unprecedented numbers. In contrast to the experience of their foremothers, they were no longer isolated individuals struggling within a patriarchal tradition: they created their own sphere of action. The subjects they wrote about, the feminist slogan "the personal is political," became the major literary theme of the decade – for men as well as women. Critics responded sensitively to the ways women's texts exploded conventional forms of genre and language, for this new "écriture féminine" (women's writing) adopted the subversive tactics of the avant-garde. In the midst of this period of intense activity, in 1975, Jovette Marchessault began to write.

Earlier, Marchessault had dreamed of becoming a writer, but suffered a block and so turned to the plastic arts instead, where her sculptures attracted immediate attention. In her first solo exhibition in 1970 in Montreal (at the Maison des arts la Sauvegarde), she showed the powerful earth mothers for which she has since become famous in shows in Montreal, Paris, New York and Toronto. Working rapidly with found objects, Marchessault puts together large, happy women, frequently photographed out of doors where they appear rooted in the soil. They incarnate the ancient telluric myth of origins, of the marriage of the sky father with the earth mother, so important in Quebec social mythology. Marchessault also paints images of cosmic harmony and creates brightly coloured masks, akin in their emotional power to those of the North American Indians.

When Marchessault started to write, she drew on the same mythological material for her two works of fiction, which are myths of origins and stories of her own coming to writing. In doing so, she initiated a new visionary stream in Quebec writing. While she draws on a long tradition of mysticism in Quebec, Marchessault changes its direction and undertakes a critique of the masculine domination of this tradition, centred, as it has been, by the sermon of a priest, representative of the Christian sky father, so that the full erotic and creative potential of the earth mother has been denied. In western culture, this female principle has been relegated to the lower, earthly realm. Marchessault reclaims for the Great Mother her earlier status as Queen of Heaven as well as of Earth. In *Comme une enfant de la terre* (Like a child of the earth, 1975), Marchessault shapes a myth of origins from the goddess's cosmic egg. When it was cracked, light and dark, heaven and earth came into being. For Marchessault, too, disruption is creation. The her-story she writes, oriented both to the past and to a visionary utopia she hopes to bring into being, disrupts patriarchal myths of origin. Her work continues to be original, creative – visionary – because it subverts and criticizes social and literary norms.

Comme une enfant de la terre is Marchessault's epic of origins, her flight through time and space to the moment of her arrival in an all-female family of grandmother, mother and girl-child. The protagonist casts her nomadic wanderings prior to her incarnation as a girl, into an hallucinatory litany of her readings, from Kerouac to the Popol Vuh by way of Katéri Tekawitha, Iroquois saint, and Mère Marie de l'Incarnation – pioneer writer and saint, founding mother of Quebec literature. She dreams of singing and shapes her vision into twelve cantos.[1] Chanting her rage for life, the protagonist relates her birth as "le crachat solaire" (the solar spit) when, from the mating of the great she-bear (Ursa Major) and the polar star, she comes into being as a shooting star. Falling to earth, she comes to reside in an all-female family.

La Mère des herbes (Plant mother, 1980), the second volume in Marchessault's proposed trilogy, continues the story of origins. Having reclaimed the heavens for women in her first book, Marchessault now sets out to expand the powers of the more familiar earth mother. In doing so, she draws on her childhood experience in a family of women. Marchessault's mother and grandmother had knowledge of traditional female healing practices and told the stories of this female culture over and over again. In seven songs, Marchessault retells anecdotes from her childhood spent with her beloved grandmother. This is the story of a writer's apprenticeship as she first grows to consciousness of the flood of her grandmother's words in a house by the river. In the final song, alone now, the protagonist settles in a house of her own by a river and her writing joins in the flood tide of women's speech, both siren's words and healing, fertile, amniotic fluid. Interspersed with anecdotes illustrating the grandmother's strength are passages which impressionistically convey the lore of the goddess, of a time when God was a woman. As chronicler of an ancient culture where woman was the centre of life, Marchessault has recreated a mythology which displaces the Christian creation myth of the fecundating divine Father's Word. This new myth locates the origins of creation in the woman's body and gives a visionary sense of what the future might be when women's power is recognized.

In terms of both its theme – the reclaiming of the role of Queen of Heaven – and its style – monologue – *Lesbian Triptych* is a part of this phase of Marchessault's development. Before discussing it in detail, however, we may gain some awareness of Marchessault's aesthetic by turning to her later dramatic works, in which she has expanded on her role as the living memory of women's traditional oral culture. In taking up the pen, Marchessault has entered a tradition of women writing. She is very much aware of belonging to this alternative matrilineal tradition and in her plays has taken on the role of its literary her-storian. Through an exploration of her work, we gain an understanding of Marchessault's own myth of literary origins, her self-discourse on what it means to be a woman writer, and a sense of the tradition of women's writing in Quebec.

Marchessault begins her task as literary critic in *The Saga of the Wet Hens* (1981), which brings together four women writers across the boundaries of time and space for an evening's discussion of their writing and a women's ritual of creation. They break bread, drink wine and dance in a circle together, before ascending into the heavens on the wings of the hen which will lay the cosmic egg. Among them are Gabrielle Roy and Germaine Guèvremont, two of the four classic Quebec novelists (the other two are men – Ringuet and Roger Lemelin); Anne Hébert, one of Quebec's foremost poets, who was a major force in introducing Modernism to Quebec literature; and Laure Conan, the first professional woman writer in Quebec and originator of its modern psychological novel. All of these women have been courageous: Guèvremont in persisting in her writing despite her large family and heavy domestic load; Roy, the nomad from Manitoba, first to write about Quebec's working class; Hébert for having shaken the literary establishment to its roots with *The Torrent*. All, too, have gone beyond their feminine condition, moving out of the solitude deplored by Hébert to express revolt, like Roy, and to paint images of women recognized for their talents, not their beauty, like Guèvremont.

Alone of these, Conan – the pseudonym adopted by Félicité Angers – failed to develop strong female heroes in her work. Yet, as Marchessault confesses in an interview, Conan is the precursor she feels most drawn to, because just by writing, by being the first woman in Quebec to have a literary career, she demonstrated enormous strength.[2] Conan defied convention, resisting the censure of church and family, by refusing both marriage and the convent, the only acceptable roles for women in Quebec society in the nineteenth century. She courted clerical blame with her first novel *Angéline de Montbrun* (1884), which centred on private passions rather than on national history, then considered to be the only acceptable subject for Quebec writing. In the play, Marchessault reveals Conan's spirit by metaphorically linking her with a horse, although she is terrified of the fires of censors that threaten her literary production. At that time, the power of the Index and the threat of excommunication were very real and invoked against writers to ensure conformity to Catholic values. In her later work, Conan bowed to clerical pressure and wrote historical fiction. While researching the play, Marchessault wrote about her aim to bring these writers out of time into the same place: "To me, they are our mothers, angelmakers or rainmakers, burned or drowned in ink.... I'm so excited – and terrified...."[3]

As literary critic reclaiming women's culture, Marchessault brings to light the work of misunderstood writers of the past and gives it a sympathetic reading at last. As in other contemporary Quebec feminist writing, Marchessault combines fiction and drama with manifesto to make the identification of an alternative matrilineal tradition perform an essentially critical function of challenging the established tradition. More recently Marchessault has extended her portraits / criticism to international writers who have particularly affected her, first in *La terre est trop courte, Violette Leduc* (1981) to the terribly lonely, addicted, tortured, self-educated Violette Leduc, with whom she closely identifies. Marchessault, like her character Leduc, is "writing her life," writing herself into existence, according to the existentialist paradigms. In her latest play, *Alice & Gertrude, Natalie & Renée et ce cher Ernest* (1984), Marchessault turns to the literary salons of Paris kept by the great modernist and lesbian writers earlier in the century, Natalie Barney and Gertrude Stein, to analyze yet again the material and psychic conditions of women writers, even as she belatedly offers them support and praise. Feminist criticism is the voice of friends touching and greeting each other. As she writes:

> There where patriarchy castrates and ridicules us, robs us of our images and our voices, and prevents us from striking out into the vast territory of the imaginary ... that is where feminist criticism and other forms of solidarity and recognition help us pursue our creative journey.[4]

Her creative work exhibits this new feminist criticism in its ultimate form – as creative writing, not formal essay.

By exploring this literary her-story, Marchessault creates a place for herself within a tradition. Through her analysis of the constraints on these foremothers, she draws attention to the fact that literature is artifice, not reality, which is socially constructed by patriarchal conventions. In this self-mirroring of the texts, she gives clues to her reader for interpreting her own work. This self-reflexive meditation on what it means to be a woman writer is a perennial trait of feminist literary discourse.

Although it is beyond my scope to explore Marchessault's place within an international context, Violette Leduc is an important figure here, for she connects the two relevant strands of writing as a lesbian and as a self-educated primitive. As Marchessault portrays in a scene in *La terre est trop courte,* where Leduc's talent is recognized by Nathalie Sarraute, Clara Malraux and Simone de Beauvoir, recognition within the tradition of noted writers was very important for Leduc, a self-taught writer. Marchessault's first affinity, documented in the two novels, is with a strand of primitive writing (evidenced in her allusions to the Popol Vuh and to Jack Kerouac, among many others), and with the oral tradition of women. Just as her coming to writing has led to her re-vision of the possibilities of this inheritance, so, too, has her exploration through drama of a Quebec matrilineal literary tradition led to its re-vision. Marchessault has drawn on this literary tradition ambivalently, making use of its long history of mysticism, even as she changes the grounds for that visionary experience.

In the outline of literary her-story which a close reading of Marchessault's work offers to us, it is clear that the potentials for female creative power have been severely limited by social institutions, especially by the Roman Catholic Church whose dominance in Quebec society was uncontested until the Quiet Revolution of the 1960s. This is the significance of the particular Quebec version of the telluric myth of origins which is most fully explicated in Louis Hémon's novel, *Maria Chapdelaine* (1915), when Maria is enticed to stay faithful to the land by the sermon of the priest and the song of the woman, both mystical voices which offer her fulfillment as a mother. The invitation to female eroticism, to the celebration of the female body of earlier versions of the myth, which consecrated the marriage of sky father and earth mother, is repressed here, when the consummation occurs in the exchange of disembodied voices. The Catholic view of the Immaculate Conception of the Virgin Mary, who in her turn was fecundated by the Word of God, determined the symbolic role of woman within a Catholic society. No longer powerful and fertile Demeter or Aphrodite, woman is celebrated as virgin or as submissive mother. Marchessault attacks this myth by excluding the repressive ghostly priest preaching God's word and restoring to women their erotic bodies.

Paradoxically, she draws sustenance from this same Catholic tradition in Quebec which has conferred such an elevated status on women, even though it has limited their social roles. And within these limitations, women did make an important contribution to Quebec society, in both its spiritual and economic development. Jeanne Mance raised money to finance the founding of Montreal, while Marie Guyon, Mère Marie de l'Incarnation, played an executive role at Quebec as founder of the Ursuline convent. Such outstanding women were also among the first contributors to Quebec literature. Mère Marie de l'Incarnation is especially important in this regard. Her letters, like the *Jesuit Relations* (also of the seventeenth century), were major documents about the founding of the colony, but from a woman's perspective. These letters also describe and analyze her religious visions, creating a tradition of women's visionary writing in Quebec on which Marchessault draws, even as she changes its meaning radically.

These early "heroines and saints" were beatified by the Church and the evolving national mythology made them the founding mothers of a matriarchal society. Women in Quebec consequently enjoyed an elevated status, more so than that of their counterparts in English Canada. Then, too, like their anglophone sisters, they were generally better educated than their menfolk. Everything would lead one to expect the appearance of "scribbling bluestockings" who would start a national literature as did the women in anglophone Canada in the early nineteenth century. But this did not happen, for what won them greater symbolic status also restricted women's social role. There was to be no recognition for them as independent career women. Only as symbolic mother or as saint – the bodiless Virgin Mary interceding with the Heavenly Father in a spiritual enterprise – was woman acceptable within the Catholic symbolic system. Until Laure Conan defied this symbolic role of women in the 1880s (though under a pseudonym), there were no professional women writers in the province.

Even then things were slow to change: a growing number of journalists started the women's periodical press around the turn of the century and published creative works as well. However, only Françoise (pseudonym of Robertine Barry) has her work in print today. Although there were some poets through the 1920s and 1930s, they were either all grouped together in the early literary histories as minor "women writers," or omitted entirely. It was not until the 1940s and the emergence of Roy, Guèvremont and Hébert that women writers became major literary figures in Quebec.

There are historical reasons for this late development of women writers. The hold of the Church over Quebec society did not lessen greatly in the twentieth century. Because it controlled secondary and university education, these were private, and families would choose to educate sons before daughters. Institutions of higher learning for women were slow to develop. This situation did not change until the 1960s, as one of the major reforms of the "Quiet Revolution." Quebec women were active participants in the suffrage movement from 1893, when the National Council of Women of Canada was founded. Some also joined the Fédération Nationale Saint-Jean Baptiste, a Catholic movement. Despite this activity, however, Quebec women did not win the vote until 1940; they had to wait even longer for other basic rights, such as control over their property, which were acquired in English Canada in the nineteenth century, and to become legal persons. These rights were not acquired until 1964.[5]

Women who came of age in the 1960s and started publishing in the Seventies were riding on the crest of an active feminist movement. Because they had been constrained in their social and political roles so long, they took up their pens in an explosion of energy. This decade of political struggle in the context of the anticlericalism of the Quiet Revolution had also made feminists aware of the enemy, woman's symbolic position, imposed by religious custom. When the revolt broke out, rage was directed at two things: at the corruption of the Church as institution, and at its ideological position which had infected the symbolic imagination of an entire province. It was time to protest against the representation of women as Virgin Mother and to reclaim the bodies of real women.

Marchessault's tremendous anger against the oppressive order of priests bursts out in "A Lesbian Chronicle from Medieval Quebec" and "The Angel Makers" in *Lesbian Triptych*. These fictions employ the satiric device of inversion, of turning the Church's teaching upside down, in a manner similar to other Quebec feminist satirists (Denise Boucher in *The Fairies Are Thirsty* and Louky Bersianik in *The Euguélionne*) in order to denounce the way in which the Church has oppressed women's sexuality.[6] The satiric denunciation of papal authority in the "Chronicle," the humorous puns on bull-Normal School, the bull-dog compulsory heterosexuality, the channel bull, burlesque the religious order, while the inversion of the annunciation in "The Angel Makers" into the blessed arrival of death, instead of birth, travesties it.

Thus, Mère Marie de l'Incarnation's influence has been erased on one level of Marchessault's work in the denunciation of Catholic orthodoxy. On another, however, her lineage is still clear in Marchessault's concentration on an inner vision. Mysticism has often been a means of overcoming existential anxiety and has been used by many Quebec women writers between Mère Marie's death in 1672 and Marchessault's work 300 years later. A major work in this tradition is Conan's first publication, *Angéline de Montbrun* (1884). This novel tells the story of a devoted daughter who goes into an emotional crisis and confinement on her father's death. The first part, a conventional narrative in epistolary form, is followed by pages of reflection on the protagonist's inner life, in diary form, prefaced with the title "feuilles détachées" (loose leaves). The title of this hallucinatory section, part prayer and part confession of inner turmoil, provides the link with more recent writers. Thérèse Tardif, in *Désespoir de vieille fille* (An old maid's despair, 1943), which explores the tumultuous reverie of a woman who has lost her lover, uses the heading "feuillets détachés" (loose leaflets) for her rambling jottings. Tardif's visionary technique, characterized by development through imagery, analysis of the psyche, and fragmented forms, links back to the prose of Mère Marie de l'Incarnation. But her style also leads forward to that of such celebrated writers as Anne Hébert, Marie-Claire Blais and eventually Nicole Brossard and Marchessault herself. In these latter writers, the eroticism of the vision of the heavenly lover is replaced by the presence of a desiring female body. The visionary mode of writing has given birth to the poetic novel, the forte of modern Quebec literature. It is in this genre that Quebec women writers have earned their greatest fame.

In the last decade, the outpouring of women's creativity has been fed by the streams of feminism. At the intersection of France and America, a new generation in Quebec has been broadening the implications of the feminist discourse from both these foreign intellectual centres. Within Quebec itself, several different feminisms are circulating. Though joined by their disruptive forms, by their being for women, rather than about women, the two resulting poetics effect their challenge on different fronts. Both challenge the notion of a central truth and the concept of origins. Both are concerned with the fact of difference, and thus develop Simone de Beauvoir's paradigm for the relationship of the sexes in the dialectic of self and other, sameness and difference. However, one is a form of feminist deconstruction, concerned primarily with the fact of oppression and with the construction of reality through language. It emphasizes the fact that there is no originating moment, but only symbolic tracings in language which may be combined in an infinite number of arrangements, may be perpetually quoted and requoted. It seeks through techniques of doubling – satire, inversion, parody and other self-reflexive modes – to expose the figures of rhetoric and intellectual paradigms wherein patriarchal discourse has established itself as the central truth.

The other stream of feminism might be called the resurrection of the feminine. It is primarily concerned with all that is other and different from patriarchal discourse, all that has been excluded from the present symbolic order. It seeks in the irrational, the traditionally feminine, a secret mother tongue and establishes an alternate moment of origins in the union of women. Rather than working on language to disrupt its naturalizing effect on us, as the deconstructionists do, this feminine writing introduces new symbolic dimensions, new subjects into fiction. Most specifically, it concentrates on translating women's sexual drives, desire that is related to the figure of the "orgasmic mother."[7] This image makes Mary's body real, and challenges the Catholic dualism which separates saintly motherhood from sinful sexual pleasure, Mary from Magdalene. This new image of woman is paradoxical, combining both Mary and Magdalene, and thus confounds the Catholic doctrine that has kept women separated from their bodies.

Birth is at the centre of this new symbolism: women's writing revises the masculine myth of origins, the Oedipal story which is parricide, where strong son kills off strong father. Instead, through her writing the woman writer makes physical contact with her mother, like Kore reunited with Demeter. She returns to her own birth, to create herself anew from within her mother's body and inaugurates an alternative lineage, her-story. Within her mother's body, she finds her forgotten mother tongue — that preverbal mode of communication which is touch or cry. If she places this encounter within a historical past, within the activities of the Great Goddess, this is an archeological venture. Should it be located in ritual, gesture in contact with the real body, it is primitive, archaic, immutable and unchanging origin. Marchessault combines the two versions of origins in her own birth in *Comme une enfant* where she descends from Ursa Major to the body of her mother and grandmother, in a union of celestial and terrestrial, goddess and real mother, reminiscent of Marian Engel's *Bear*. And she does so again in "Night Cows" when she flies high into the Milky Way on a mythic apotheosis even as she explores the body of her mother, become that of a sister, in an erotic lesbian embrace. Indeed, in the period when she was completing *La Mère des herbes,* and "Night Cows" and *Saga* were being thought out, Marchessault wrote about the corporeal reality of this mother tongue:

> In the last few days, what a rush of images, as if my memory were surfacing, the memory that was mine before my birth. My mother talking to me and talking to herself when she was carrying me in her belly ... and this monologue stimulating me on every level. I believe this monologue was my introduction to the essential flow of language....[8]

Marchessault's emphasis is on the contact between real bodies rather than on retrieving the missing link with the historical goddesses, and she is responsible for introducing this theme to Quebec literature. This was evident in a special issue of *La Nouvelle Barre du jour* called "Mermour" (pun on motherlove), which she edited and where she first published "The Angel Makers." In this feminine aesthetic, the Word is made flesh of woman's body and the emphasis is on the surfaces of the body, on the cry, on a wealth of experience that has remained always on the other side of language, in the realm of bodily experience — menstruation, childbirth, and lovemaking, especially between two women. In attempting to name this silent experience, women writers inject new themes into literature through the venerable theories of Romanticism which emphasize the importance of strong emotional experience as a source to be translated into words and become literature.

On the other hand, the deconstructionist feminists who concentrate their attention on the surface of the text, who attempt to make the flesh word, emphasize that words are never a translation of experience, never mirror reality. The only reality is the writer's pen which inscribes her libidinal energy on the page and the reader's muscles which turn the page. The Quebec feminist deconstructionists work within a tradition of Modernism which emphasizes the autonomy of the work of art, its nonreferential nature, the inability of language ever to mirror some extratextual reality. Here the sacred is in language itself as the writer-shaman plays with words, "deconstructing" them, detaching them from the odours of theology still present, though as thealogy, in the female shaman's quest for the feminine.

Both modes of feminist writing invite a new sort of reading experience based on sisterhood. The opacity of texts where the feminist deconstructionists play with received meanings requires a reader who will become a coparticipant in the creation of meaning as she actively works to make sense of their textual puzzles. In reading the feminine texts, we are invited to fill in from our experience as women to give meaning to the new themes of the biological body, based on our long unverbalized experience of them. It is the feeling of recognition of this shared experience which gives meaning to the experience of reading about women's lives. Through this process we literally construct our own lives.

Many permutations and combinations are found within these two broad directions of feminist writing. The major mode of deconstructing the figures of the patriarchal symbolic system is the carnivalesque parody of the received institutions of the Church and psychoanalysis which we have become familiar with in the work of Louky Bersianik.

She is building on the work of Claire Martin and Marie-Claire Blais who denounced the misogyny of the Church in satiric attacks in the 1960s. This deconstruction may also take the form of the play on the material reality of the book practised by Nicole Brossard and Yolande Villemaire. This is inspired by Marxist theories of the material production of the text. Brossard, especially, disrupts the concept of the book in order to prevent it from becoming a consumer object and the reader from becoming a passive acceptor of ideas. She emphasizes the physical processes of reading and writing, continually blurring the boundaries between the book's fiction and reality when her narrative self-reflexively comments on the movement of the pen across the page. The real bodies of the writer and of the reader are brought into play in the white pages that allow time for the reader to turn to other matters outside the text or to turn the page.

Within the feminine aesthetics of the flesh, we may observe different tendencies under the broad heading of psychoanalytic approaches. The one celebrated by Madeleine Gagnon in "Mon corps est mots" is influenced by Lacanian reinterpretations of Freud in which woman as sign is absence because of her position as the other, that is, as the object of discourse. She is unable to go through the separation from matter necessary in order to become a subject and to speak, because she does not separate from her mother in the Oedipal complex. According to Lacan, woman does not exist: she is excluded from the production of symbols and meaning, and is nonsense. But as such, she is radically different from the masculine subject, and challenges his preeminence. The foundations of this masculine discourse about man's experience as subject are called into question by the new subject matter introduced by the feminine aesthetic: the bleeding, lactating female body, a spelling that comes once a month, a writing in the white ink of mother's milk, as Hélène Cixous writes in "The Laugh of the Medusa."⁹ And Marchessault picks up on this white writing in "Night Cows," in the image of the mother's milk, to produce the fluid, associative, irrational writing that is the characteristic of this feminine writing, and is opposed to the rational linearity of masculine discourse.

In affirming this difference, however, these writers are still caught within the definition of the "eternal feminine" as it has been used to exclude them. They are defining themselves as men have defined them, close to body and nature. Moreover, by framing this definition in psychoanalytic terms, they run the danger of perpetuating it forever. Privatized, this experience cannot enter the public domain as her-story. Cixous herself announces the advent of feminist writing in the future perfect in a moment after the feminist revolution, introducing the necessary connection with history, with society, needed to escape from biological origins. This mode of utopian distanciation is used by writers like Marchessault to posit an ideal, feminine world where women's difference will be valued in and for itself, not denigrated as it has been under the patriarchy.

Though this silence in itself may be a form of renewal, and must thus be thought of as a form of revolt, as Madeleine Gagnon suggests, there is another form of revolt that moves one out of the silence of the human body.[10] To cast this woman's culture into a social form, into a lost historical reality, rather than into shared rituals of the biological body, is to open it to possibilities for change. This is a direction that much American feminism has taken, exploring the lost matrifocal cultures of Celtic Europe, the prehistoric Mediterranean, and North American Indians. Jovette Marchessault's archival digging, which she catalogues in *Comme une enfant,* places her work within this mode of feminine writing, rather than the neo-Freudian one. Her revival of the lost feminine becomes a form of feminist archetypalism. The historical element of her feminine aesthetic has been reinforced in her plays which, heavily researched, bring to light the lives of historical figures marginalized by the dominant culture. Marchessault's interest in this feminist archetypalism introduced it to other Quebec women writers. Thus, their work differs from the neo-Freudian direction of French feminist thought, concerned to combat the repression of the feminine, and is closer to the Canadian current of feminism, concerned with the expression of the feminine. Although Marchessault is alone in Quebec in reclaiming a native heritage, through the Indian ancestry of her beloved grandmother, she has collaborators in English-Canadian writers like Margaret Atwood and Margaret Laurence, who have linked the creative muffling of women with the ideological oppression of the native peoples. To give voice to the concerns of the muffled native cultures is to find an original creative voice. However, Marchessault's closest kinship is with the painter/writer Emily Carr, who forged a unique artistic style from her contact with native perceptions of the wilderness, then transferred her direct and emotional approach to create an innovative literary language. Carr's Klee Wyck, the laughing one, and Marchessault's shooting star share a gyn/ecological imagination (to use Mary Daly's term), which relates the rediscovery of the muted feminine to the development of a perspective which respects all that has been perceived as the Other in western civilization.

Marchessault's work is situated at the intersection of feminist discourses current in the international sphere as well as in Quebec, and the texts collected in *Lesbian Triptych* are located at the crossroads of the critical and celebratory functions of these discourses. The critical function dominates in "A Lesbian Chronicle from Medieval Quebec," which uses parodic inversion to indict the institutions of death, the Church with its cannibalistic and sadistic "Immaculate Copulation" and its communion, in which a girl is forced to participate, first rite in the death of her body. Her indoctrination to submission is carried out through sermons that depict woman as "the evil of nature painted in bright colours." Father's Word covers mother's body completely. Here Marchessault quotes scripture in a new context that effectively exposes its misogynistic, even pornographic nature. The girl-narrator also rediscovers the hidden body. Contrasted to the assault by the priest's word is the idyllic relationship with nature celebrated by the two girls romping on a farm in Ontario. But the protagonist's beloved "day cousin" turns into an unknown "night cousin" on the arrival of her boyfriend. Then begins a mute, death-in-life courtship which culminates in the mourning of the cousin's marriage by the two girls. This story of the conforming child, who fulfills patriarchy's destiny for her — death of the self — is opposed by that of the rebel who resists the movement into adulthood, trying to hang on to the natural world as she dances through the seven veils of Church doctrine (the seven deadly graces/sins), throws them back in the face of authority, and walks herself right off the sidewalk of this world into a woman-centred world. This is a poetic chronicle of a girl's growing up and coming out as a lesbian. Marchessault's wit is rapier-like in its punning on the images of religious authority and underlines the way in which power has been exercised to kill women. Here Marchessault follows in the footsteps of Quebec women writers of the 1960s who denounced the Catholic Church's preference for the mummified body.

"The Angel Makers" introduces a similar death/life conflict in order to denounce male "rights" over women, which include the rights of the blood (that is, the rights of the first night), rights of reproduction, and birthright. In a pattern of satiric inversion, Marchessault's woman emerges from the uterus in a left-turning position. Left-handed, i.e. "sinister" (from the Latin), therefore a criminal, she is also left behind. But it is her powerful and paradoxically creative left hand, the mark of her difference and deviance, strengthened by knitting, which takes the unwanted fetuses from their mothers' wombs and wrests back that reproductive right for women, the right to choose. This fiction depicts the traditional female creative activities of knitting and cooking to give a new image to the "angel of the home," no longer submissive, but active as abortionist. The traditional mother was an ironic figure of death-in-life, while the new death-bringing abortionist is a giver of life, an "angel maker." In this, "The Angel Makers" combines the satiric critical discourse attacking patriarchal values with an expressive, feminine one.

"Night Cows," the central part of this triptych, is the pivot, introducing the utopian vision of a world of women beyond patriarchal constraints. Here they float on the Milky Way displacing the heavenly father from his sky kingdom. The foundations for "Night Cows" have been established in the "Chronicle," which also plays with the difference between a day cow and a night cow. In "Night Cows," night and darkness are a time of freedom and celebration, not the prelude to death, nor the time for prostitution as in the "Chronicle." As well, the narrator of the "Chronicle" has imagined the wonder of mother/child connections should lesbians give birth to babies without male gynecologists. These babies would have only a single idea in mind: "to suck at mummy's breast, to swallow all the stars in the Milky Way, to soar away, to float, to burp.... " Marchessault expands this image of ecstasy in "Night Cows" where it becomes the grounding metaphor. In the company of the trickster crow, the docile cows who sweat by day in the kitchen are transformed at night into creatures of beauty, into sisters whose bodies give delight to each other.

"Night Cows," the transition between the two sections of the book, is also a turning point in Marchessault's writing, away from fiction towards the theatre. "The Angel Makers" was intended as part of a long fiction; the "Chronicle," too, is clearly a narrative form. All three texts are monologues, the basic narrative form of the oral tradition that has given birth to Quebec fiction. Recording the Quebec folktales to prevent their loss, writers in the nineteenth century produced the first short stories. More recently, writers like Antonine Maillet have evolved complex fictions from oral stories, a practice Marchessault follows in her long fictions where she gives permanency to her grandmother's tales. Monologue has also been the basic form of Quebec theatre, especially of feminist theatre.[11] Following in this tradition, "Night Cows" is the first step in Marchessault's theatrical career, leading to the more complex characterization and dialogue of *The Saga of the Wet Hens*.

In *Lesbian Triptych,* we have only the dramatic text and not the theatrical text, a fact that poses a problem for the reader, for there is a tension between the two. The one we read is ethereal reverie, seemingly devoid of any action. In Pol Pelletier's performance, the extensive imagery of the active tongue and the pulsating rhythms of the prose find incarnation in her gestures. In the performance text, both visceral and ritual elements of theatre are emphasized. The limited stage props — a stool — foreground the activity of the female body which occupies the entire theatrical space. There is also a mask of a long-horned cow placed beside the stool on which Pelletier sits in her black leotard. This mask is put on during the transformation of the day cow into the night cow. Through this code of costume, Pelletier emphasizes the ritual nature of the performance, returning to the Greek origins of theatre through the masked actor, but with a difference that is all the meaning of Marchessault's text. For this is not the story of Oedipus in tragic masks that we are attending, nor even the Dionysian rituals that give birth to tragedy, but the Eleusian mysteries with their accent on female eroticism and celebration, evoked through the horned beast symbolically associated with the holy grail and the moon, and thus with the rites of the goddesses. In this play, as in *The Saga of the Wet Hens,* we see concrete evidence of the great swerve or break in the western literary tradition which is promised by this feminine myth of origins. [12]

Marchessault's theft which becomes flight of imagination is in turn parallelled by Yvonne Klein's in her fine translation. In the operation of transcoding a set of meanings from one language into another, it sometimes happens that things are radically revised. Meanings may be lost, in this case the context – the place of *Lesbian Triptych* in Quebec feminist thought, its allusions to genres and texts not necessarily familiar to an English audience. However, it also happens that meaning is gained in the process of translation. For example, we have the rhyme in the "Chronicle" of "choke" and "bloke," which is more effective in suggesting the connection between men and violence than the French "choke" and "chum" (though the fact that these two words appear in English in the French text emphasizes the imperialist as well as patriarchal oppression). We also have the wonderful discovery of an equivalent for Marchessault's "Saigneur" (which combines the French word "Seigneur," liege lord, with "saignant," bleeding) in Klein's "Leech-Lord." In its new context, then, Marchessault's text continues its work of appropriating and subverting received meanings. Like the night cows, it flies away with language. [13]

NOTES

1 The musical mode is important for Marchessault whose grandmother made her living as an accompanist for a circus and for films. One of her position pieces is entitled "It is still impossible for me to sing, but I write," (*Jeu*, 16 [1980], pp. 207-10). My translation.

2 Donald Smith, "Jovette Marchessault: de la femme tellurique à la démythification sociale," *Lettres québécoises*, 27 (automne 1982), p. 57.

3 Jovette Marchessault, Letter to Gloria Orenstein, *Saga of the Wet Hens* (Vancouver: Talonbooks, 1983), p. 14.

4 Marchessault, "Foreword," *Saga*, p. 8.

5 Bill 16, granting women these rights, came into effect on July 1, 1964. For further historical background, see *L'Histoire des femmes au Québec depuis quatre siècles,* by the Collective Clio (Montreal: Quinze, 1982), forthcoming in English from Women's Press, Toronto.

6 Denise Boucher, *The Fairies Are Thirsty* (1978), trans. Alan Brown (Vancouver: Talonbooks, 1983); Louky Bersianik, *The Euguélionne* (1976), trans. Gerry Denis, Alison Hewitt, Donna Murray, Martha O'Brien (Victoria: Porcepic, 1981).

7 Julia Kristeva, *Des Chinoises* (Paris: Editions des femmes, 1974). Kristeva has gone on to expand on the importance of maternity in offering a new symbolic order in "Women's Time," trans. Alice Jardine and Harry Blake, *Signs,* 7, No. 1 (Autumn 1981), pp. 12-35. She rejects Freud's affirmation that the child is a symbolic penis. Instead, women experience pregnancy as a "radical ordeal of the splitting of the subject; redoubling up of the body, separation and coexistence of the self and of an other, of nature and consciousness, of physiology and speech," the separation necessary in order to become a speaking subject, and the female equivalent of the Oedipal complex in the construction of the symbolic order. Moreover, mother love, with its "attentiveness, gentleness, forgetting oneself," is a different experience of otherness from fusion in sexual passion, and offers a model for difference in which radical difference does not automatically lead to the suppression of the other (p. 31.).

8 Marchessault, Letter to Gloria Orenstein, *Saga*, p. 12.

9 There is an echo of Kristeva here. Hélène Cixous, "The Laugh of the Medusa," in *New French Feminisms: An Anthology,* ed. Elaine Marks and Isabelle de Courtivron (Amherst: University of Massachusetts Press, 1980), p. 258.

10 Madeleine Gagnon, "Ecriture, sorcellerie, féminité," *Etudes littéraires,* XII, No. 3 (décembre 1979), pp. 357-62.

11 Laurent Mailhot, "Le monologue québécois," *Canadian Literature,* 58 (Autumn 1973), pp. 26-38. See also Louise Forsyth, "First Person Feminine Singular: Monologues by Women in Several Modern Quebec Plays," *Canadian Drama,* 5, No. 2 (Fall 1979), pp. 189-203.

12 Harold Bloom, *A Map of Misreading* (New York: Oxford, 1975), p. 33: "I prophesy though that the first true break with literary continuity will be brought about in generations to come, if the burgeoning religion of Liberated Woman spreads from its clusters of enthusiasts to dominate the West. Homer will cease to be the inevitable precursor, and the rhetoric and forms of our literature then may break at last from tradition."

13 Cixous, "The Laugh of the Medusa," p. 258. The word "voler" in French means both flying off and stealing and sums up the two facets of Marchessault's writing, the visionary and the satiric.

★ ★ ★

Barbara Godard is Associate Professor of English and Women's Studies at York University. She has published widely on feminist critical theory and Canadian and Quebec women writers. She is also a translator: These Our Mothers, *a translation of Nicole Brossard's* L'Amèr, *appeared in 1983. She edited* Gynocritics/Gynocritiques: Feminist Approaches to Canadian and Quebec Women Writers.

for Pol Pelletier

A
LESBIAN CHRONICLE
FROM MEDIEVAL QUEBEC

IN THAT PERIOD in medieval Quebec, lesbians competed with beings from outer space for sheer horror value. They were even in competition with monsters from the European Middle Ages.

What they knew about us was indeed monstrous: a fragmentary, crude knowledge, a knowledge which mixed the ideas of those in power, obsessional frenzy, and the bric-a-brac of Catholic ideology. There was also a kind of dirty curiosity born of boredom.

If they bothered to think about our real physiognomy, they would rapidly cast us in the conventional evil mold: repulsive, putrid, hysterical, morbidly deviant. Lesbians are substandard, they said, rejects both inside and out! They have been for a long time. Forever, in fact. As far back as man can remember, since the first word was inscribed on the black tablet of patriarchal and biblical amnesia. At that time they fought us through the politics of silence and contempt without ever pronouncing our names.

If the minister of immigration at one time agreed that the Christian community might include lesbians, it was only on the condition that we remain anonymous, that we remain wholly mute regarding our vicious tastes, and that once and for all we lesbians render ourselves invisible. To this end, motivated by concerns of efficiency and prodded as well by an acute opportunism, the minister of immigration, after consultation with the president of the Catholic multinational corporation and its virtuous members, decided to proclaim three bulls.

★   ★   ★

These very spiritual bulls were to enlighten us lesbians and help us, finally, to hoist ourselves to the level of worthy representatives of the great Judeo-Christian culture. These bulls would straighten us out and pacify us permanently. In the north, the rather restless pack of extraterrestrial lesbians were to be dispersed as quickly as possible and directed towards the confines of mediocrity particular to those times.

First Bull: Normal School. The bull-dog. All lesbians six years of age and over must enroll so that they may hear, see, and understand as early as possible all that is normal and universal. Certified dialectics, guaranteed for life. In normalizing school, the lesbian subject will learn rapidly to disguise herself as a real woman, strapping herself into the costumes that master tailors make for her. She will learn to sequester her desires, suppress her nature, throttle her spirit. She will learn to identify with the heroines of the good old international repertory, to disguise her face, her corpse's grin, the expression of disgust or revulsion that she wears so spontaneously. All this to negate her vicious lesbianism.

The Second Bull: the institution of the family. This one is a bull-dozer in a big dose. Say hello, make nice-nice, be a good girl, devote yourself to your daddy, to your dear doting grandaddy, to your dear great-uncle, your dear great neighbour, your dear great pastor. You already know those recipes by heart – and remember your dear great-brother, your dear Great-Spirit-spouse.

At the familial institute, the order of the day is: Lesbians of Quebec, smile at your stew pots, smile at your toasters, smile at your kettle, smile at your (unloaded) battery of pots and pans, smile as you iron the dishcloths, smile at your cookbooks with the recipes written for ascetics on a permanent holiday. Smile at your broom, your mop, your garbage can. Life is beautiful!

Oh, lesbians of little faith! Unnatural women! Egostical monsters! How dare you circulate the unfounded rumours you do? How dare you whisper that the sheets of *our* beds look like shrouds, that they smell of corpses, rotted meat, and open sewers? The trouble with you is that you've got both feet in your own septic tank. Get back to work. Roll up the sleeves of your gorgeous disguise and get to work. To work! Don't mock the Holy Bull of the familial institute again. It is there that your future lies. The courses we give will contribute to the

dissolution of your ego, to an integral dissolution, an hypnotic efface-
ment. But smile! Smile at the French buttonholes and at the needles
you use to knit your own muzzles. Smile at the Russian salad and the
Chinese chop suey. Poor, preserved, and pickled women, soon you
will be admiring the body of your firstborn son in his pretty little
peasant-point dress. Salad dressing, mayonnaise, white sauce and tar-
tar sauce.

The Third Bull, the Channel Bull. Burl-esque, the optimum bull
for modest lesbians. This is the perfect, paradisal bull which puts you
into death's orbit, which stifles you and constrains all your spasms of
agony. In the context of medieval Quebec, the Channel Bull, Burl-
esque, swallows down one glory-hole all the little services that lesbians who have been pacified, lobotomized, mastered, and neatly
framed have rendered from time to time to the beloved community.

When she is too old or too tired or too depressed, she joins the
diaspora of cheap lesbians who bob like corks in the dirty water, floating and sometimes going under – waitresses, both on the ground and
in the air, charwomen, cooks, housewives, streetwalkers, unem-
ployed lesbians with no place else to turn.

★   ★   ★

In order to ensure the widest dissemination of the Bull-dog, the
Bull-dozer, and the Burl-esque, the president of the Catholic multinational corporation and the minister of immigration developed a
strategy. It was simple but most efficient. They jointly launched a
recruiting campaign. As a priority, the minister of immigration
would actively concern himself with the extraterrestrial lesbians who
had recently arrived in the city. Loads of them were arriving every
day, women from somewhere else who did not yet speak the language
or who spoke too many languages. During this time, the Catholic
multinational corporation would recruit the lesbians in the countryside by twisting their arms. A spatial, partial mission of salvation.
Remember! Remember!

I do, I do remember, each Sunday, every Sunday of the year,
thundering from the height of the pulpit, the voice of the archpimp of
the village, the sole keeper of the harem, who incited us in his

Gregorian tremolo to submit. Submit, he bellowed. Submit, he terrorized us. Submit, he promised, or watch out for the bulls. The Bull-dog will bite you. The Bull-dozer will flatten you. The Burlesque will hold you up to ridicule. Those who clutch the skirts of the archpimp will be redeemed. The Trinity of the Holy Bulls swears it on the head of God the Father.

Remember! Remember! They recruited us the whole day long, century after century. On the church porch, in the nave, in the choir, in the baptismal registers, in the depths of the baptismal fount, in the dirty pocket of the confessional, as we knelt with the family to say the rosary, in the utter blackness of the night, in the depths of the fear of our own black misery, in our isolation, our solitude, in the stigmata we bear as a consequence of the Fall, in our nostalgia for a lost paradise, in the death of our hopes.

They recruited us. They hauled us in by the scruff of our necks.

★   ★   ★

In those days, I was a very little girl, but one who saw everything and heard everything.

My genetic inheritance from my mothers saw to it that I still had a damned thick knot of resistance in my memory, in my womb, and in my heart. In fact, all I had with which I could counter the fanaticism of the Three Bulls was my resistance. *They* noticed it right away. They knew I couldn't rely on my family, who were already militants in their ranks, and still less on my normalizing environment. So, in order to ridicule me and diffuse my resistance, they aimed themselves at me, the little extraterrestrial lesbian monster, talking night and day about *real* resistance: the resistance of others.

They showed me a panorama, a history lesson for the ignorant. The resistance of the Holy Apostles, what about that, eh? How about the resistance of the Christians in the lions' den, in the swimming pool of boiling oil, on the bed of nails, eh? The resistance of the French from France, the English from England, the Japanese, the Chinese (or Chinks), the Jews, the Redskins (or Savages), eh, what about them? They were ready to dig up examples from two thousand years of history. And they were exclusive models, very convincing. No, really, my puny resistance carried no weight, I ought to be aware of that. What was I, an idiot, a loony, or what? I would never get anywhere with my stubborn resistance. I must accept it: for me there would be neither epitaphs, nor decorations, nor monuments, nor the recognition of my country, nor a pension for life. Resistance was really for other people.

I understood it all.

The more I heard, the more I was persuaded … to the contrary. I heard a series of arrogant lies which they were attempting to graft cold onto my body, to graft without any preliminary anesthesia, or almost none, they were so sure of themselves. These were perfect lies, just as some crimes are "perfect" crimes. As long as I understood clearly that my resistance would at best earn me a couple of microscopic lines in the obituary columns of their newspapers, and that, in any event, I would be buried under an assumed name – the name of my daddy or my dear husband. The Tomb of the Unknown Lesbian.

They picked the wrong time, really the wrong time, to discharge their load of crap. They came too late – I had already experienced a complete illumination in Ontario, on a beautiful farm in the promised land, inside a shed. It's been many months, but I will have it in my memory forever.

★   ★   ★

In the month of June, my family in Montreal put me on a train and I left to visit that side of the family which lived in Ontario. What would you expect? Thanks to breathing all that good city air, not to speak of listening to everyone thundering and spitting at me, I had developed, according to those who know about such things, a shadow on my lungs.

One morning, a beautiful morning lit with a wild and savage light, when the calls of crows and migrating geese rang from the skies, I was sitting next to my uncle on the front seat of his Ford. We were going to the village of Embruns to get feed for the cows and pigs, and lamp oil. My cousin had asked us to pick up a yard of pink ribbon for her. I was watching my uncle: first he turned the key, then he let in the clutch. Then he made a little automatic gesture – he stretched his hand absentmindedly toward a little knob which he pulled toward him. Odd, but I had never noticed that gesture before.

"What's that?" I asked, pointing at the mysterious little knob. The starter, the accelerator, the brakes, compression, decompression, I knew all that stuff off by heart. Even the spark plugs.

"What, that? That's the choke."

Astonished, I looked at him and made him repeat it.

"What's the choke for?"

"It regulates the gas. In French, people sometimes call it *l'étrangleur* – the strangler."

★　★　★

The words exploded in my head and in my stomach. He continued his explanation in two languages and I repeated under my breath: choke, *étrangleur,* choke, *étrangleur.* He could have gone on with his technical explanations till he ran out of breath, but I didn't hear them; I could listen no more. I was in the grip of an etymological intuition, a linguistic and phonetic illumination. I began to see clearly, to put together the pieces of the puzzle. I shrank into my corner while he started the car, let in the clutch, and followed the road to the village.

I believed I had finally understood the peculiar behaviour of my cousin, her doubleness, her fits of catalepsy on the porch almost every night after seven o'clock. I had two cousins – a day cousin and a night cousin.

★　★　★

My day cousin was all life, flying limbs, and projects involving the dog and the calico cat, eggs, and swallows' nests under the barn roof. She had her nose into everything all day long.

Listen, really, she would invite me to take a little run down to the well. We'd come back walking on our hands. We would turn somersaults in the haystacks and stop indefinitely for fits of crazy laughter, hysteria cramping our toes. Breathless, we rested on one arm, our bodies cleansed of their deafness, our nerves attuned to the sounding board of our song and our joy. While we were there, we would tease the big steer who was sleeping standing up. As he awoke, he would line us up, slobbering grass, delighted at this unhoped-for visit, and thunder after us. We were far enough ahead by then to run flat out, enthusiastically cheering him on. There was lots of time to wiggle through the fence before he could gore us.

We would go to the end of the road to pick strawberries, high cherries and ground cherries, blueberries and raspberries when the rooster crowed from his barrel, or at any time, depending on the sweetness of the air, the dawn moon, the noonday sun, or the signs we read in the clouds. We would trot the whole way to the Nation River. The perch with their great round eyes looked like sibyls, the sunfish were veiled in bubbles. We would float, we would swim, taking all the time we needed to get to know the algae, the warm currents.

My cousin talked to me. She chattered away from nearby or from the top of her manor, with the whole landscape of her early childhood behind her. She spoke of everything and of nothing, of those nothings which are exchanged in the glances of young girls and which end up harmonizing in the flood tide of ferns, reeds, water lilies, and the songs of birds. Since the beginning of summer, she had been telling me a story so beautiful, so captivating, that each time I heard it, I was completely overwhelmed, inexhaustibly overwhelmed. Even today, when I think about that tale, I experience a renewal of energy as if I lived again in my childhood.

It was a tale about creatures who came from the navel of the Earth. It was a tale which had nothing in common with Snow White, Sleeping Beauty, the Star Fairy, Little Red Riding Hood, or any other fairy tale. These creatures measured four barley-corns high and four oat-kernels wide. My cousin said that they weighed only as much as a leaf and that they came out only at dusk when the wind dropped. They came to the surface of the earth to spread dew on the grass. Each had on her head a lake of blue water and, strapped to her hips, a flask of eau-de-vie, the flask whittled from the pith of a tree. They carried knapsacks containing all their food: bread, salt, and clusters of fruit. My cousin said they sprinkled dew on the leaves and fields with great sea sponges which they dipped sometimes into their blue lakes, sometimes into their flasks. That was why things tasted so good and full of juice, according to my cousin. From one day to the next, she added delightful events to her tale, details which warmed my heart. And I was seized with a deep affection for these creatures who came from the navel of the Earth. She often stopped and stretched out flat on her stomach to show me proofs of their recent passage: by the side of a ditch I could read an unusual movement of the grass, a greenness unsubmissive to the sun.

★ ★ ★

After supper, my night-cousin would go up to change – pink dress, pink ribbon in her hair, a morose expression on her face. When she came down, she was not the same. A disturbing person, my cousin!

I dogged her steps, following her outside onto the porch; sad, I asked her a hundred questions. Are you ill? Are you tired? Are you sad? Have I done something to hurt you? She would raise herself from her torpor long enough to give me an impatient shake of the head and then sink back into her lethargy. I saw her grow dim. It was terrible. At this distressing spectacle, I was the powerless audience. I would sigh heavily to attract her attention. No response. Sleeping Beauty had more animation. Slowly, slowly, she rocked, staring vacantly ahead, her hands limp in her lap. I would buzz about like a horsefly. I was persistent. I wasn't about to give up. She rocked. She waited. I hoped for a sign from her that she was still the girl she'd been a little while ago.

At the stroke of seven, I saw her boyfriend, her bloke, appearing at the end of the road. He came up, sure of himself, plunked his bum down on the next chair and gave me a look so black that in principle it ought to have killed me outright or made me leave in a hurry. He slipped his hand into hers and the evening began. It always lasted three hours, from seven till ten, practically every night. That bloke of hers didn't say much. When he hadn't opened his mouth for some time, she would ask him a question about his work or his family. Around nine, she would get up to fetch him a glass of lemonade or a cup of coffee. He drank it slowly. She gazed at him. He would say, "The lemonade is cold." Or he would say, "The coffee is hot." She would nod her head. On the evenings on which he felt particularly chatty, he would pass a remark or two about the weather. At ten, without even looking at his watch, he would get up, muttering, "See you tomorrow." She would nod her head, her eyes blank. "Yes, tomorrow."

Her bloke! Her choke! After my illumination, my etymological intuition in the shed, they were, for me, the same thing. They had the same function – to throttle.

That evening, when she had taken her place in the rocking chair, her eyes blank, I attacked.
   "You're waiting for your choke," I said guilelessly.
   "My bloke," she quickly corrected.
   "Your choke."
   "My bloke."
   "Your choke, your choke, your choke!"
   "My bloke! Have you gone deaf by any chance?"
   We faced off, red, our voices trembling, rising to a shout. Oh, she was so beautiful, so alive, at that moment. Just as she was in the day-time, full of games, full of fire, full of imaginary tales. I wanted to make it clear to her, to explain about the little knob, but the choke we were actually arguing about was already rattling the porch with his seven-league boots. He suggested, crudely but firmly, that I take my stupid foolish blabber somewhere else. I cast a last look at my cousin, hoping for support – she was already cataleptic. The next day, she absolutely refused to reopen the question, threatening to ignore me for the rest of the summer if I insisted on talking about it. Worse, she would stop telling me stories about the little creatures as tall as four barley-corns. So I stopped picking on her.

⋆   ⋆   ⋆

That autumn, when I got back to Montreal, their newspapers were filled with the horrible story of women strangled in a big American city. With photos to back it up. The entire police force worked around the clock in vain – the choke was still strangling. Respectable citizens were eyeing each other warily.

As the story went on and on, in order to keep up the interest of the people of the city – Boston, I think it was – in order to give them something to look forward to and reduce the general apathy, since sometimes several months would elapse between stranglings, the papers resorted to dredging up old stories out of the archives. Yet one more time, we had the Vampire of Dusseldorf, who admitted killing thirty victims ranging in age from five to sixty years old. Then there was the Butcher of Hanover, who had accounted for an even dozen. There was a clutch of torturers and maniacs, both obscure and celebrated. There was Jack the Strangler, as we call him in French; not too well named, since he disembowelled much more often than he strangled. He was a thief as well, stealing here an ovary, there a uterus or a length of intestine, cutting off his victims' breasts and leaving them on the table. There was also a list, shorter, it's true, of men whom they called the "lovers" of dead women. Necrophiliacs, as a matter of fact. In short, we read about nothing but demented, repulsive acts.

This series of murders seemed quite energizing at the time. All sorts of theories surfaced. Among others, one maintained that sadistic crimes, essentially committed for sexual reasons, were always the work of men. The discovery of the century! To their joy, the Boston Choke was arrested a few weeks later. The scholars, all the most educated men, made a mad dash to peer at the genital logos of that deranged strangler. They drew the most astonishing conclusions by beginning with irreducible biological facts. After months and months of effort, of intensive research, consultations, seminars and banquets, they succeeded in dredging a Y chromosome out of the seminal mud. Then came an historic announcement – only chokes seemed to possess this Y chromosome. They began again, reanalyzed everything, but there was nothing for it: the Y chromosome brings about a mutation in the strangler which is completed just before his birth. Another declaration: this Y chromosome leaves an indelible trace in the choke's brain, in his medulla oblongata, particularly in the area of the hypothalamus, which controls the competitive drive in the normal strangler through the action of the pituitary gland. They held, as far as I could make out, that a choke in action is a frustrated athlete who compensates for his loss of sperm through a little fit of strangling or a judicious slashing or a mortal blow. The choke's need to strangle, they concluded, is inscribed in the entire race of Cain or, if you prefer, in its genetic potential.

★   ★   ★

I, the little extraterrestrial monster, certainly landed on earth at a great time. These were difficult times, and their solar calendar didn't help. They hadn't had a lunar calendar for a long time, since a certain Julius Caesar, in fact. Some conspirators rushed to the senate to kill that divine personage, not because of the calendar, of course, but anyway, it was too late; the dictator had finished his work.

The first six years that I spent here in this north country, in the full force of medieval Quebec, were especially hard on my cells, my intelligence, my sensibility, my sense of space, and my need for love. I could understand nothing, but absolutely nothing, about their damn calendar. It was all Latin to me! I was always late for a feast day, for a saint going into his tomb or another one coming out in an odour of sanctity, for a crown of thorns, for a fight to the finish with the Archangel of the Principalities, for a prophetic curse, a plague of Egypt, for a flight, a deluge, a Last Judgement, for a horseman of the Apocalypse bearing pestilence, or for a celebration of a beheading. I always missed the last prophet who had just turned the corner of the Wailing Wall in his fiery jalopy. If I dared, I would say that their liturgical solar calendar looked like a strangler's noose or like a giant ploughshare which tore apart and worked over my poor daily life in the promised land.

When they spoke of feast days, when they said "Feast," I heard something else. I heard the bloody winter across the Land of Men. I heard grief, suffering, and bottomless descents into despair. They said "Feast," and I heard guilt, punishment, redemption, permanent sacrifice, a flight into nothingness, humiliation, flagellation. The banner of the final pardon at the end of time was scissored out of my very skin. They hoisted my carcass in the paradise of the future which marked an end to my days. The supreme commander of the warship reached out his arms to me and smiled at me from afar, from his station in the blockhouse.

Feast! Feast! Those traps designed to complicate matters; it was so loud in my ears I was almost deaf. That's why I was always late for a feast! I was so behind that the rumour got out that I was backward! So freaked and hunted was I, the little lesbian, that they said I was a freak.

At the vernal equinox, for example, they took advantage of a season as soft as a peach skin to trip us up with the voluntary sacrifice of a super male come to redeem us. Focus on the victim – men are always the victims, and women are responsible – and not a word about what is going on over our heads, about the breezes which are aroused, about the horizon which springs up, and especially about the Moon which fights against the shadows at this time of the year.

That struggle, that genuinely cosmic struggle in the galaxies, those amorous golden lightning bolts, the clamour of the skidding comets, the springs of the greatest beauty which water the stars. A struggle which lasts a fortnight. Two weeks of sound, colour, odour, mad vibration, desire! A period which sees the Moon waxing in the heavens, marshalling all her quarters, before deciding once more to dedicate herself to the Earth, to her new life cycle. Two weeks! Just enough time for the Moon to birth spring over the world. The fiery soft fruits, the astral seed, the leafy forests, the greedy little mouths, the texture of our skin, the wild grasses, all of these the Moon perfects, preparing them for the marvellous voyage they will make toward a pool of water, a hollow in the earth, a mammalian womb.

The lesbian calendar has nothing to do with the solar-liturgical-Roman calendar. With us, it seems to me that everything is accomplished through desire. With us, to desire proves that we are doubly alive. Desire is a grand, irrational invasion which liberates more and more joy. In desire, we know we are united, that through us courses the memory of our grandmothers, the hearts of our mothers. It is nourishing beyond belief, beyond all logic. With us, it is desire which prevents neutrality from taking over. Each of us knows that when she feels desire, she is summoning up the words of all the others like herself, the words of the women who sow, the uninterrupted words which shoot across the beds of time in phosphorescent arrows.

*   *   *

Shock waves through my entire body, waves of fear in a little pause between two corrections, and I was suddenly on the verge of tears. I was barely five when I became suicidal. There were two departments in the process of giving me orders and administering me. My family was responsible for keeping me in line. I was the perfect excuse for a particular myth of politicians and policemen which, with beating drums, carried on the intensive manufacture of normal women. After meals, my family invariably told me, "Go play outside." A sibylline sentence.... "Outside," in their language, meant on the sidewalk. Without fail, they always added, "Take your skipping rope." That way they were sure I would stay in one place.

On the sidewalk. Not in the street. Not in the lane.

Skipping in place on the sidewalk, I could take the time to be aware of and contemplate my luck, which I did, but the wrong way, against the current somehow. Beyond the history I was being taught, I could make out another history with which I could begin to align myself. I refashioned the creation of the world my own way, out of immediate particulars drawn from the memory of another world and my cut-rate memories of the earthly paradise.

In the beginning was the street, I said to my skipping rope. The sidewalks came later, after Daddy-God had divided *his* forces of light from the darkness. He delegated Cowboy Jacob, Cowboy Moses, and Cowboy Elias to park the forces of darkness in a particular place in *his* promised land. Cowboy Jesus and Cowboy John the Baptist christened the place: they called it sidewalk. Along with the noun sidewalk, they created the verb to sidle, which means to slip along. The shadowy herd sidles along the sidewalk, mares and cows sidle, bitches sidle, mice sidle, women sidle. Sometimes, even the imagination sidles!

One day I experienced an irresistible desire to set one foot in the street, once and for all to get my initiation to life on the sidewalk over with. A fantasy, a momentary aberration – no one is perfect. I could already hear in my mind the whistling of the big switch that would raise welts on my back whenever someone in authority became aware of my insolence. The cowboys were firm about it: there must not be a single little girl in the street, or the shadow of a woman. An overwhelming experience, confirmed a thousand times by tradition. Watch out!

I stuck one foot in the street.

What a curious sensation! Here was a blank slate, a whole world to be populated! I stayed in suspense, one foot in the street, my face tense, expecting the worst. Nothing happened. The rest of me followed my foot. Bliss! Joy! Gasp! I walked a step, my knees still knocking, my back hunched to avoid the blow of the switch that could not be long in coming. Nothing! On the contrary, passers-by turned solicitously toward my little self. Considerate drivers stepped on their brakes to let me pass. To let us pass, that is — me, my skipping rope, the bottom of my pink underpants, and my big lollipop. I felt I was the queen of the pampas confronting an enormous landscape.

But there was my daddy passing by....

I tried to explain to him that, for a little girl, the street was almost totally safe: the consideration, the solicitude of the people. Nothing doing – he turned a deaf ear once again, not wanting to hear anything about my experience, my line of argument. A voice inside me said that in this town – or anywhere else – if a driver were to squash a child, a riot would break out, the cowboys would howl, lynchings would take place. Compared to what I had submitted to on the sidewalk by way of the squashing of my desires, my needs, being squashed by a car seemed simple, almost innocent!

★   ★   ★

A little while later....

I was turning seven. Either to punish me or because they had no choice, they sent me to school.

"She must make her First Communion," they said.

After being in the Land of Permanent Sacrifice for more than six years, I was further and further from everything – from myself, from the sweet central memory of the other world, from my body. Mossy death was gaining on me. I was getting rusty all over. After six years of being broken in, I would finally make my First Communion.

There ought to be something better to talk about.... When I think of that year, I am still stricken with a kind of shame.

All the little lesbians in that period in medieval Quebec were sticking out their tongues and drooling on the floor or on the pictures in the Shorter Catechism. After the Feast of the Magi was over, they decided to make us submit to intensive training. We were the fetishes of the year, the pigs' heads with the gold rings in their snouts, the monsters. The planning! The premeditation! The furious anger! Until they had completely exhausted our unceasing resistance. They put the accelerator to the floor just to extract one word of agreement, one genuflexion, one bow from us.

"It must be done," they said.

We were filled with so much perfidy, so many ravaging demons! Right away we heard the old saying: "'Femina' comes from 'fe' and 'minus' because a woman always has less faith and retains it less." Saint Isidore said that and the good bishop added: "There is no malice like the malice of a woman." And Saint Chrysostome, embroidering the text of the Apostle Matthew: "What is woman but the enemy of friendship, an ineluctable sorrow, a necessary evil, a natural temptation, a desirable calamity, a domestic peril, a delectable scourge, the evil of nature painted in bright colours."

They made us swallow this ground glass and threw in on top of it a throatful of prayers and hatred. It was a mutual hatred, because I hated them as much as they hated me.

Don't think for a minute that they had their great organs thunder for us. Certainly not: all we had as background noise was the piercing little tinkle of a bell: ding! dong! ding! dong! It made my hair stand on end. Ding! dong! ding! dong! It drove us crazy. I was ready to lick the filth from all their cult objects just to stop the noise of that little bell. Ding! dong! ding! dong! The heavenly hosts, ding! The glory of the Father, dong! The sacrifice of Junior, ding-a-ling! The Holy Ghost, with his ferocious dong! For whom the bell tolls, dong!

They were preparing us for Holy Communion in the form of a kind of unleavened bread, white, dry, stiff, and hard. It was white enough to gouge out my eyes, so that I felt my sockets were like my head — empty. It was so dry, it cracked my lips; so hard, it made me sick. All the little monsters were sweating with fear, trembling on the springboard over the abyss, dizzy, their thousands of red-hearted cells furiously contracting, refusing the Immaculate Copulation. But we would not be allowed to refuse; we would be taken care of and in short order.

Oh, miracle! Oh, prodigy! A great round white host replaced the sun in the skies of our winter days.

Just a minute now! Pay attention! Lesbians, whatever you do, don't touch the sacred host with your dirty hands. That is absolutely forbidden. You will be punished; you will go to hell. Don't touch the host with your sluttish hands. That is not done. That is never done. Even in the days of the first Christians, when ordinary males took communion themselves, in their own houses, in the catacombs, the women had to cover their hands with a white cloth so that their dirty bitch-skins would not even brush the immaculate-host-containing-the-immaculate-kid-of-the-immaculate-mother-who-conceived-in-one-ear-and-gave-birth-out-of-the-other.

Not for one minute were they ashamed to tell us all their dirty ideas. They even forced us to learn them by heart. Don't touch the host with your dirty hands, only with your tongue. Receive the host on your tongue in prayer, meditation, humility, and renunciation. On your knees, ding! dong! On your knees, little girls! This is the exquisite moment of divine fellatio. On your knees! Open your mouths! Wide! Wider! Receive the great eucharistic male's jet of sperm. Are you in a state of grace? Have you not eaten? Have you brushed your teeth? Don't let the sperm effervesce around your wisdom teeth too long. Swallow! Swallow the sweet Jesus; let yourself go; let yourself be penetrated by his divine mercy! Allow yourselves to be sown with the seeds of his bounty. Let yourselves be irradiated and purified by him!

Pay attention now! Don't imagine for a minute that it makes no difference who receives that subtle sperm in their wide-open traps and who experiences that same little thrill in their mouths, in their taste buds. Nothing could be further from the truth! It is all codified, regimented, and anticipated.

For example, women who are completely crazy may not take communion, except for those rare moments when they are in their right minds. Otherwise one would run the risk of irreverence, either toward the host itself, or toward the virile member of the clergy who put the host into their mouths. My dear sisters, pornography is everywhere!

In the case of women who are deaf, dumb, and blind from birth, they may in no circumstances have access to the Eucharist because clearly these women lack understanding.

Suicidal women, those whose minds are so bent they can think of nothing else but throwing themselves against a wall or beating their brains out with a chamber pot, repulsive creatures like these cannot, under any circumstances, ask to receive communion in public, out of the respect due Junior's sperm.

They thought of everything! They had the delicacy, the refinement, the sense of hierarchy which shits all over you.

Although I didn't know it ahead of time, in February of that year I was going to live through my first week of holy afflictions. It was a week which began with Ash Wednesday, followed closely by Treason Thursday, then Good Friday with the three-hour death, the ejaculations of Saturday night, and the flabbergasting resurrection on Sunday. The last week of Lent, week of weeks! Everything devoted to the cult! The army of preachers sicced on us by the Catholic multinational corporation finally caught up with us. They rose up in their pulpits to launch their imprecations, steaming up the windows, drooling tuberculous spit, the same old story, a stream of piss to gulp down for your health. Not a moment to lose, but eternity to win!

In medieval Quebec, the churches were full to bursting. They were doing a land-office business. Ding! Dong! Cash!

The multinational Catholic army was in first-class shape. Those holy week preachers had the vigour of athletes. They wooed us little lesbians with their fatal frenzy: with snips of their scissors, tightenings of their nooses, hooks to the left eye, they made mincemeat of us. I was hamburger, tripes on the prie-dieu; there were only scraps of me left – bits of ears, nose, and mouth. With a final stroke of a plane over my skull, they scalped me of my imagination, just to hold it up to the redskins. The preachers leaked their homicidal gases. Was there any chance at all that one day the light would shine over this enormous ratatouille, this human meatball stew, this tender nursery of epileptic babies? One after another, we submitted to the outrage, the goosings, the aggression, the rape, the promise of resurrection.

I tell you they stole our ordinary life from us.

Our precious ordinary life, when we could play inside, outside, or upon the green grass of our mutual tenderness. They stole our life with others like ourselves, our fiery life of red velvet passion, rocking in ecstasy in our bodies' embrace. They stole our high noons under the branches of the Mother-tree-in-flower, next to the fountain flowing with the transparent water of our mouths, with the moist kisses which become acts of acknowledgement. *"Il y a longtemps que je t'aime, toujours je t'aimerai."* They stole our time to drink by the sea.

When I think of it! Whenever I think of it! I want to howl, I want to kill them. But at the same time — the emptiness of it all. It is a permanent tragedy; every minute of the solar calendar celebrates a sacrifice according to Mosaic law, a holocaust. No matter how much blood flows, the Father's thirst is never satisfied. The same underlying fantasy rotates around a fixed centre, blood runs, blood drips in visible waves from the tips of the knives of the just, who are their Father's kids. Moment by moment, we have martyrdom, heroism, sadism, fanaticism, and waste of life. "Men are the victims, and women are responsible," as it was already said.

Try to picture a multitude of human beings, the overwhelming majority of them men, bubbling away in the horrible heat of a great vat of boiling oil. You'd expect a mixture of despair, cries of pain, death greeted with relief.... Not a bit of it! You don't get the picture. In their vat, the martyrs are plunged into a state of extreme concentration: some of them are wrinkling their noses as they reflect upon their past sins; others enjoy themselves by removing each other's heads; others castrate themselves; others crumple up their faces singing hymns.

Oh, how quickly I learned about pain!

Pain is a wave which carries everything along — dreams, desires, visions, the creatures who came out of the navel of the Earth; it is a tidal wave, a knife which cuts me to the heart to sever my bonds to life. Primal pain! The more it hurts, the more primordial it is. They taught me to love that fugitive pain. Our profound, almost incurable, visceral appetite for pain. We wind up believing we were born with this appetite, this taste, because it twists our guts, it makes us fat; it fills our heads from ear to ear.

Little girl, there is no better way to self-actualization. It is even worse than that, more horrible; it fills your whole being: to become one whose bowels give way, whose bones crack, whose morale and high spirits are destroyed by the file which rasps the nerves, the saw which saws away all resistance. Womb-scraps harden on the floor. You are flushed with the freshness of the first cloud you encounter in your state of levitation. You're on your way to seventh heaven. *Fulgo fulmina,* please hold off the lightning bolt, remove desire from me, and its fiery mother. *Congrego clerum!* Convoke the clergy, quick, quick, here comes the parade of crusaders who are filing into the hub of the commercial centre of total abnegation. The hour is come to fulfill the seven last words of Christ, that soapbox orator, his papa's son.

* ★ *

I learned an awful lot growing up!

I learned any number of salutary truths!

No more fooling around: from now on, I would achieve my significance through religious faith. The coup de grâce! I learned my triple curse: shame, sin, and torment. I am not making any of this up. I could not possibly make it up.

The First Curse: "The curse of shame awaits women who never conceive." – *Genesis*, in the version authenticated by the Catholic patriarchy.

The Second Curse: "The curse of sin awaits those who do conceive" – that's what little David said to Goliath – "I was conceived in sin." When dear little David speaks of sin, you may rest assured that he was talking about his mother's womb.

Third and last Curse – in their system, everything goes by threes: "You will bring forth children in sorrow." – *Genesis* again, in the version most widely circulated, number one on tradition's hit parade. The curse of torment will await all women who give birth.

There was my grandmother Elizabeth who conceived a son in her old age ... and of course my cousin Mary, who also had a son ... and then sister Rachel, who gave birth to a son ... and Eve, who had two sons ... and there was Judith ... and Sarah....

But how come all the women in the Bible only had boys?

They thought that was a sensible question, their kind of question. They spewed forth their one-way answer. Isn't it obvious that the God of Hosts has to intervene down there – "down there" evidently meaning the womb – because my womb is merely an incubator with walls made of bloody flesh, clods of dirty earth and a little salty water. Without the intervention of the Holy Ghost, not one little speck of life could spring into being inside that bag of skin. Of course it is he, with his fiery kiss, his fecundating tongue, he, who is passionate and fulfilling, he, who is perfection within the law, he, with his generous tongue of flames and his ruffled feathers, he, who is the saviour of lost causes, the notary of our lost heritage, the indulgence in the year of jubilee, it is he who grants me the seven graces in the blink of an eye.

He is agile, acrobatic, quick to propagate himself; he works miracles in the miserable wombs of women. The babies which our mothers manage to put together without his magical assistance are foggy splotches, leftovers to go into garbage cans. Women's work is badly done; it is a cut-and-paste industry in a little underground workshop. Cheap labour! Look at yourselves! Look at me! Am I not the living proof, the prodigal daughter, the poor in spirit whose mother made her all by herself without the intervention of the Holy Ghost: no forceps, pliers, scalpels, hooks, knives, tongs, or a caesarian operation helped this fetus be born! Unbelievable! Miraculous!

Imagine for a moment thousands of women, thousands of lesbians engaged in the production of babies in overcrowded conditions, in badly heated dwellings, with excessive hours of copulation. Imagine the bawling, defective infants, born without imagination, with only one idea in their heads – to suck at mummy's breast, to swallow all the stars in the Milky Way, to soar away, to float, to burp to touch, to laugh, and at last to fall asleep in mummy's arms. You can imagine what the result would be if Old Flame-Tongue, the super-gynecologist, was not around to shape all those babies into saviours and sufferers, redeemers and olympian gods!

★   ★   ★

It's crazy, but I feel I am being manipulated.

It's crazy, but I feel strangled, scorned, discredited. It's crazy, but I feel spied upon and detested. My brain cells are being raked with fine steel combs. It's crazy, but I feel I have been short-circuited, disconnected. I am becoming sad. I am becoming morbid. It's crazy, but I am in the process of going crazy. I'm cold. I'm afraid. I am being punished. I am never right. I am regressing. I am panic-stricken. Whom can I say this to? Who will grant me even a little credibility? If I speak, are they going to demand to see my proofs? Say what it is you have to say! Calm down! Be nice, be sweet. Listen! Listen carefully to what you are about to hear. That's an order!

What else is there to do but listen, unless you want to puncture your eardrums or open a vein while munching on tranquillizers?

I listen. The saint-phonic orchestra is playing me an air identified as Gregorian. According to their experts, no greater music has ever been created. No stricter unity has ever been imposed on sound! All its themes concern religion, so there is no fear of any weakness of inspiration. The vocal art is sacred, as it is conducted and sung by men sworn to chastity.

If you feel that Gregorian chant is a tiny bit ambiguous, maybe the barely disguised and sublimated expression of male homosexuality, that's because you are a bit bent yourself. Or maybe you're jealous, even envious. You'd like to mingle your voice with theirs and you can't do it. An organologist, or any ordinary organist, will tell you that your voice is naturally polyphonic and that voices like yours have been banned for a good thousand years from sacred music. The incendiary Papal Bull John twenty-two, Council of Trent. Music is the prerogative of priests, angels, choirboys, and eunuchs. So Saint Cecilia is the patron saint of music? That's only an accidental error, a youthful aberration. Anyway, she is always shown playing the cello, an instrument which didn't even exist in her day.

Only the masculine registers have the keys to the city in Gregorian chant. For this chorus virilis, the first note is always an eighth note, in unison, cantus planus, that is, in the unmodulated tradition. No triplets, no feminine emotions, nothing to seduce the ear, no softness. Gregorian plainsong is insipid monotony written for Adam's apples capable theoretically of two diatonic octaves without emotion.

They wanted me to dance to their tune. What an inspiration for me! Come on, come on, they say – show us what you're made of. The great singers have their eyes trained on you. The great musicians are waiting for your trance. This is no time to masturbate or keep your clit under glass: we will have your entire attention. Come on! One, two, three, one, two, three – one step forward, two steps back, three steps back, and begin again. One, two, three, one, two, three. It's easy. Shake a little. Give us a few visions, some excitement; they're our daily bread. Let yourself go to the rhythm. Let that serpent, that sexy viper, that immutable nymphomaniac slither in your juices. It's great to be cut in two; it's great to dance the way you're going to. You're going to ascend to heaven quicker than I can say. Ascend to heaven, young virgin, one step back, two steps back, three steps back, ascend, ascend straight to heaven, yes yes yes, absolutely. Good lord, you're talented! You'll be a great star, a great soloist dancing a unique dance. Whatever you do, don't panic. Trust us. We are here to help you and guide you. Don't panic – you have all the time you need to repeat and perfect your withdrawal. You have your whole life ahead of you.

Females made of tears, blood, and coloured clay in yellow, red, black, grey, white, and green. Every woman will learn the dance of the seven veils.

Accepted everywhere, it is the passkey, the free pass, the passport. The saint-phonic orchestra has its eye on you as it has its eye on all the demonic women – mothers, bacchantes, sirens, particular friends, medusas, harpies, enchantresses, angel-making abortionists. All the mad women will dance to the holy score of the dance of the seven veils.

Seven! Like the seven carnal sins, Junior's seven last words, the seven plagues of Egypt, the seven years of the lean kine, the seven sacraments, the seven commandments, the seven gifts of the bird of paradise. The four Horsemen of the Apocalypse plus the Holy Trinity: that makes seven. The four evangelists plus the three theological virtues: that makes seven again. Always seven! The seven days of their week, the seven notes of their scale, the seventh heaven of the seven planets of their solar system. Seven, like the age of reason. Seven, like Septuagesima.

After that feast day on their calendar, they schedule my time, checking that I am making progress. I dance seven times a week, in fair weather or in foul; I dance to that music which envelops me in its canons. I mark a little time on dry land, then my star-dancer's body is outlined against the blue of the ethereal spheres. I dance, I dance. I have it in my blood. Even if I lapse, I have it in my blood and in my memory, and in the aqueducts of my ears. That Septuagesima is hot stuff for me, the lesbian.

They called this a period of deviation, a time of exile and tribulation. The order of the day was *Circumdederunt me gemitus mortis,* the moanings of the dead have surrounded us. But I made them uneasy. I disturbed them. Something was eluding them. What was it, they asked themselves. This question was making them crazy. They could not manage to define the problem. Was it my appearance? My gestures? The position of my feet? There seemed to be something un-Catholic about my dance! When you dance, they asked me, what are you thinking about? I don't think about anything, I answered. I think about the dance, that's all. They went into the room next door to consult and to prepare their attack. They felt I did not have the proper expression on my face and that everything else was slightly out of whack; that despite all my gifts, despite all the passion I brought to the dance, despite my promise, despite my consenting thigh under the indiscreet swelling of my belly, that despite all this, I lacked an inspired mind. But I could have confidence in my choreographers – they would fix it. They returned inspired. They outlined for me the general theme of the seven choreographies on a bit of paper.

From that time forward, I danced my haunting dance in homage to the seven honourable names of Junior.

On Mondays, when I danced in honour of Junior, the Doctor, they advised me to perfume my body, to wash all my nooks and crannies, all my dirty places, longer than usual. On Mondays, then, I danced for the Doctor.

Tuesday was the day of Junior the Redeemer. They recommended that I adopt a certain stiffness of expression, an air of admiration in my smile, a few discreet sighs, a few languorous movements. On Tuesdays, I went two steps back for the Redeemer.

On Wednesdays, they suggested I get down to it, put on my white gloves, my blonde wig, hide my total, fatal flesh under my pink chiffon. On Wednesdays, I was expected to go three steps back for the Liberator!

Thursdays — feast days! days of glory! They ordered me to inhale the white vapour which rose from the inexorable incense of the obsessions of a ferocious clergy which celebrated a black mass in burlesque of the white. They asked me to admit that I had signed a pact with the devil, that I had eaten meat on Fridays, that I had never set my sights on the perfection of sainthood or of martyrdom, or on canonization in the long run. On Thursdays, I danced for the Denunciator!

Fridays, oh, Fridays! They were exhausting! I had to recapitulate everything from the first day, right from the beginning. They advised me in the kindest possible way that my bodily movements were often rather bestial. How that revealed my inadequacies to me! These weaknesses had driven me to regrettable, unpardonable extremes. How could they put up with me any longer if I didn't improve my style? On Fridays, two steps back for the Boy Scout!

On Saturdays, I outdid myself. I ran through my repertory several times, I reached all the way down to the bottom of my bag to make room for controlled improvisation. I gave myself absolutely, I exploded out of my navel, my asshole. I protruded from the pores of my skin. I was the music tamer, the keeper of the locks, she who breaks eggshells with her great sabbath sabots, she who chews her voice twenty times before singing, she who still takes the time to graft a byzantine fineness onto her dirty, lascivious movements. There I was about to light up my eyes, a voluntary torch, just as a distant relative of mine, Salome, once danced before drowsy old Herod. On Saturdays, I went three steps back for the Voyeur!

On Sundays, Salome or not, I did not have time to call for John's head or play the role of castrating woman. The time had come for the uterus of Christ — he would give birth to the golden age, the iron age, the steel age, the age of reason. His people were hailing him. His father was calling for him. Tight-an was about to ascend to Heaven. Earth bored him. Tight-an was fed up and disgusted with our vices. Tight-an would leave nothing behind him, not so much as a dried-up turd for the carrion crows. Tight-an was taking off and I fell at the feet of colossus, fainting, speechless, my armpits dripping. I knelt, I prostrated myself before him, who was bleeding me white, our very own Leech-lord.

To put it another way, I was dancing for nothing, for free; I danced for their glory, not my own. I was dolled up in rags. Poor little impure girl, my crevices which held the matriarchal splendour of eternal red female pulsations made me dirty ten times over. I lost my life in those patriarchal dances which were merely analogues of embalmment. I had no time to catch my breath, to dry my tears, to lean my back against the wall. Once again they would give me a shove from behind to put me back into orbit in the pearly celestial spheres of the Catholic rainbow. They forced me to enter their arks of the covenant rising under the porticoes of their gothic cathedrals.

Evidently, I am not to receive all those seven veils at the same time. Ah ha! The narcotic is carefully doled out.
    They begin modestly enough with just a little veil end, the baptismal veil. I'd like to bet that no one ever feels it resting lightly on her face. Such lightness! Its colour: the neutral shade of an earlier body of a pure spirit detached from the rocks of its chastity. A polished, made-up spirit, well equipped to save me from my original straitjacket. Its little moaning voice casts a shadow over my being. It breathes its fetid breath into my mouth; it lays down a regimen for me which I would have to follow to the letter, with the help of a kick in the ass, if necessary. The second veil? It is of an identical texture; only the proportions are different. The penitential veil — already it is more cumbersome. And the others? The third, my First Communion veil, and after that, the one I wore at my confirmation, and after that the bridal veil. The sixth is the nun-virgin's veil, worn by the pasha's superannuated wife. And the last, the grand finale, gleefully tucking me in, is the ultimate veil of the Last Judgement.

The obscurity which sets in after the third veil is the most horrifying and the most demoralizing. I knew that my sight was faltering, that as one veil after another descended, the light would become more and more feeble. The light would fail, that unforgettable light of Earth, the light of a smile, of a glance, of the mixed essences of love, friendship and tenderness, which together relieve the blackness of moonless, solitary nights. Moreover, I saw I would never have the time to learn braille. That was out of the question, no permission would be granted and no time. My happy homemaker fingers would be kept busy tidying the dark house of my depression. They would sharpen all that was round and harden all that was soft and tender. They would work the family cult objects – those piercing-pinching-cutting-slicing objects: clothespins, diaper pins, meat knives, scissors, crochet hooks, knitting needles, embroidery needles for cross-stitch, and knucklebones for the game of human procreation. I'd get a thimbleful of murky water to slake my thirst. The only other water for me would be dishwater, wash water, sludge from the pipeline which is plugged directly into the brains of retailers.

And I danced. Oh, did I dance! Can't you see me? I danced in the shadow of innumerable archways. I danced through the sky blue enamelled doors of tabernacles. I went up in smoke before the slender charm of the calyx-chalice. I shrank like an earthworm before the flamboyant gold plate on the sides of the ciborium.

I danced! Christ knows, I danced!

⋆　⋆　⋆

When I wasn't dancing, I went to the neighbourhood school, a kind of grey zone, a folding bed for the proletariat. Time passed, I grew older, produced crowsfeet and wrinkles, and slowly shrank, huddled into a corner of myself. The hive of my failures and my concessions burdened my mind.

During the intermissions, I went home to my mother on Mentana Street. My mother, the common lesbian, was the lady-in-charge, the special agent delegated by Central Intelligence to supervise the day's end, the evenings, the sleepless nights into which I was plunged by nightmares, my dawns and early mornings. She was responsible for overseeing my development on the household dance floor. They had furnished her with a whole outfit so she could carry out her job: a manual for the complete and frustrated animal trainer, free internment in the home, radio-meals-husband laid on, numerous pregnancies, lice, cockroaches, bugs, mumps, and hemorrhages. The house on the lost continent of Mentana Street swallowed us more and more, us with her.

Cannibals, stop the ball!

I was ripe for a conversion by force. The more time passed over my head, the more invisible I became. The lesbian I had been became so invisible that the angels in the Bible were more real than she was.

In this era in medieval Quebec, practically everyone could furnish an exact description of an angel, without ever having seen so much as a skeleton of one of these pure spirits. But when it came to us, the lesbians, there were only rumours circulating, rumours full of insinuation and slander. Lesbians? Lesbians were sick, neurotic, vicious, aggressive, bitches, syphilitic and arrogant. Their pathology was characterized by left deviationism. Totally left. What a horrible thing for a woman! Shouldn't people like that end up being killed? I believe that they used to burn them in the good old days. No entry. Danger zone. Lesbians, you are requested to slow down. Stop! Stop! Red light; we are about to enter the legal male parking area.

It was at least seven years since the great male Eucharist had squirted his sperm into my mouth. It was time that I developed and accepted growing up, time that I stopped defending my body, which was too big just for me. What kind of possessive egoist was I? Red light, red light, red flood, what was happening to me? Life was making me dizzy. This is my body, this is my blood, that precious concoction, a frenetic warmth, the gurgling of liquids.

Little Red Riding Hood, daughter of the red mother, is requested to surrender herself to her proprietors.

Heterosexual? Lesbian-homosexual? You haven't a clue, my dear proprietors, my dear surgeons! You try to graft your obsessional weakness on my body and on my head. Your grafts present certain difficulties, however. You see, they result almost always in weak beings who kill each other, rack their brains and everything else. Neither hetero nor homo, my dear obsessed sirs! I am in another place, in the forgotten zone, in the no-man's-land of women's memory, the ah!-my-zone, my first land, that incomprehensible continent of desire, before which you fly into a rage, brainsick, terribly troubled in your original sin.

The great primordial goddess survives here, she who is all-beautiful, the vast grandmother of Earth and sky. It is she who maintains the ultimate watchfulness in the memories of women. She washes our memory with the beautiful waters of birth, of survival, hope and innocence. She restores our interior order, anterior to desire. That damned desire must have been constructed to divide the waters of our mothers, so clear is it.

Homosexual? Heterosexual? My dear proprietors, I am autosexual. By taste, out of solidarity, continuity and premeditation. I am guilty right down to my ass. Mine is an iconoclast's hand, a living fragment, as monosyllabic as your Gregorian chant. But I have no illusions. I know there are not too many of us autosexuals. I am a survival, a survivor of the patriarchal concentration camps. Among the little girls in my class, there are not too many autosexuals left to bear witness to the proprietors' crimes against humanity. But I promised myself that one day, one day, I would speak out loud, memory by memory.

You would say to me, you hypocrites and threateners, "Evil to her who causes scandal." Your little angelical-evangelical phrase has dragged around in my head for a long time, with its fearful vibrations, negative to the point of death. That phrase made me sweat, piss, shake, and shit. Each time you knocked at my door, I would think of the Four Horsemen of the Apocalypse, I would think of your courts of judgement. I would be afraid. I am afraid, but I choose to keep on living and to keep on speaking. These words may break down the separation between women. Power and oppression must some day come to terms with this book.

There are no oubliettes made to fit me in the death-system of medieval Quebec. I keep on speaking.

I was made autosexual and autosexual I remain. I can also remember that at one time, at least half my class was autosexual. The little first-grade girls held out pretty well. After the third grade our ranks began to shrink: there was an epidemic of normality, a famine of self-love. We had not been vaccinated. Vulnerable in this way, we were at the mercy of the first Wise Man who came along. By fifth grade, after we had made our confirmation, it was almost a desert: my classmates, my childhood loves dropped like flies. After seventh grade, it was all over: Sleeping Beauty fell into her beautiful sleep, hopelessly drugged. There was nothing left but sexuality for my childhood friends, the friends of my girlhood: the auto was in the control of the proprietor.

They were enclosed inside the panoramic vision of males who would launch them on a dead-end trip. They were catapulted into the world of one-way traffic, of the agonizing squeal of tires. Automatic transmission from father to son! Heirs to the throne, to the ignition key which starts incest, rape, conjugal rights and beatings.

★   ★   ★

Here we get to an interesting age, here we get an age characterized by perpetual dismantling, maximum misdirection.

Have you seen their swollen autos parked head to tail the length of the streets which surround the local school? Have you looked? They are the pack, the army, the invaders of the army of love-by-force, of the army of the quick fuck. They are the knife-wielding runts, the hit men of our vices. You shouldn't miss the show, the solo-monologue performed by weirdos. They sit there meditating, the little cherubs, with one foot on the accelerator, one hand in a pocket, the other picking their noses, ready to lift us up and lead us at last out of our inertia, out of our lethargy, out of our contemplation of death, out of our contemplation of the remote. From this moment on, right away they are the objects we must contemplate and go on contemplating, until we single out just *one* for contemplation. Our lives belong to them and everything that goes with them. Hurry up, big girl; cut here, cut down there, my dear; cut up above, cut down below. Cut off your language, your imagination, your visions, your intuitions. For me you must cut the cord which still connects you to the milk cow's great belly. Pooh-pooh! Aren't you ashamed, at your age?

We have arrived at an age of significance! An exciting age! Oh, the beautiful little girls, the little whores, the lure of fresh meat, warm blood for Count Dracula-of-the-hysterical-incarnation. Our heroes are exhausted. Our heroes tilt back their heads and stretch out their hands to Me: just one! Just once, and afterward you can leave. Just one little transfusion to set me up and put me back in tune. One time, that's not going to kill you, for Christ's sake. The lure of fresh meat, a premature ejaculation in the front seat or the back seat of the big Canadian Ford-made-in-the-u.s.a.! Since they have the proof between their legs, they are sure and certain that they can put us into orbit and make us waltz toward the regions of permanent sacrifice far above the Earth. Too bad for those who doubt, for those reluctant ones who don't care for the itinerary that the king of creation has mapped out for them. These auto-conquerors are so faithful at their posts: every school day at 3:30, they delicately line up their cars around the school. We are encircled. They light their cigarettes or pipes and whistle an air from La Traviata, or Carmen, or Auprès de ma blonde, or the danse macabre, or the shark's fox-trot. Patient. They are all on the same wavelength, with the same poison in their gullets and identical mold growing on their faces. These melancholy, stale-smelling rapists, these grandpapas in drab suits would do us the honour of choosing us as they might a chop off a butcher's tray.

Tssss! Tsssss! Tssssss! Tsssssss! No, that's not a rattlesnake.

Tss! Tssss! No, they're not merely picking their teeth with their tongues. Tss! Tsssss! Oh, what a miracle, what a marvel, they've just spoken my name! Tss! Tssss! That's me, that's me, maybe it's you too? Tsss! Tsssss! It's really me, my Christian name, my family name and all. No matter what you say, they really do know something. I wonder how they found out. Tss! Tsssss! They envelop my heart and my body with my new identity. This is truly self-realization. Tss! Tsssss! How content I am. At your service, gentlemen.

What I had to put up with in the form of physical and-emotional mistreatment! They sprang to the attack, those males, with haggard looks, their teeth chattering, spitting in the dust of Genesis, pinching, cracking jokes, ready to fuck. Making out in chaos, they shoved their smelly torches between my hands or into my mouth. They looked at me as I passed: Misss Tsss! Tsss! They licked their chops as they saw me walking by, a walking Adam's rib. Good enough to eat! I heard them sharpen their teeth, I heard their mouths watering, I heard them drool as they took out their sharp and pointy tools. They would devour my eyes, suck my marrow, gnaw my bones, strip off my skin. They wanted to cook me in the oven with their radioactive mushrooms. Oh, what a nice piece! A nice piece of meat!

What do you expect when we have passed our lives in a community which sanctifies cannibalism: "Eat thou and drink — this is my body and this is my blood." "This do thou in remembrance of me," added the Sandwich Islands cannibal, the Christian ogre.

There are certain months in the liturgical year when they dress up as hunters and turn their gaze in another direction, looking for other game. What fun it is to blow a bird out of the great river of air, or to assassinate an elk where it stands, or drown a fish in the grass, or spill the blood of any mammal as it springs toward the freedom of the woods or mountains! They go other places and kill other things, but it's only a substitute, another of their subtle little tricks. No matter what they do, the clay woman will always be the target of their sinister farce.

They are everything! Everything at once: pioneers, good samaritans, heroes of the last western or war movie, patriarchs, prophets, confessors, policemen, informers, protectors of widows and orphans. It is simple enough — you look at them and they change before your eyes. How do they do it? Osmosis? Symbiosis? For the latest male avatar, with his gonococcus, his urinary troubles, his soft chancres, the female vagina acts like a septic tank, the public dump at rush hour.

Of course, there's never a question of these heroes inviting Misss Tsss! Tsssss! to a hotel or a jolly brothel. Everything goes so much quicker in his big Ford Meteor. It's faster, more practical. Eat it here. There isn't a trace left. No tipping. You can do it in the wink of an eye and you can make a quick getaway if things don't go so well. An orgy on the sly, while the Saint Christopher medals dance in the whirlpool of the great failing wave which would submerge us. Saint George and the dragon. Poor Saint George, his scapular is caught in his fly.

Don't touch my relics, my chalice. Don't touch them. You think that's funny, eh? You forget that's what they are – relics? My relics are my head, arms, legs, vulva, tongue, and every part of my body in which I have suffered, provided that that part is reasonably large and complete. I am a living relic, from the top of my head to the soles of my feet. So put your frenzy and your little punches and your undertaker's fumblings where they belong. I am a visible scar, an ancient burn mark. Do not touch my body again without my full consent, without my total desire for a night of love with you! Back off a little, back up. Odd, but I smell something funny and it's coming from you. I smell you. You smell of the trap. You smell of the iron bar. I can't help sniffing out a professional plot between you and the torturer. You smell of the mercenary, the boss, the headsman, the straitjacket, of electric shock by lightning bolt.

Misss Tsss! Tsssss! will not be the servant of the Leech-lord who bleeds her white!

When I was fourteen, I knew clearly, sharply, lucidly, that I was never going to turn daddy on, whether living or dead; not doting Daddy, or Daddy-God-the-father, or Daddy-Adam, or Daddy-Buddha, or Daddy-Mahomet, or Daddy-son, or Daddy-brother, or Daddy-Christmas. I was still terrorized by Daddy-hairy-split-and-bearded, but I will never agree to masturbating him or sucking him off. Not even if they wash my brain one more time. Not even if they threaten me with the sword of Daddy-Damocles.

After fourteen it will be too late for me to grab what is left of my life and make off with it. It is now or never to separate, since everything is going by so very quickly. I suffer from a shortness of heart, tears, fears, the bloody writing on the too-autobiographical page of life which is published blindly. I grow older. I advance at breakneck speed toward the marital age, the conjugal complex. I hear all the rumours of desire aroused by my body, by the breadth of my hips, the size of my breasts, my ass which they yearn after. Yum, yum, they lick their lips and bare their pointed fangs.

I amaze myself at having so much strength in my body, so many projects in my imagination, and so many, many desires. More and more, my desires come to resemble my twin sister, myself, whom I admire. We are inseparable. Belly dancer, womb-dancer, soloist who dances the iniquitous dance which means little to me, when I look inside my imagination, when I see the smile therein, the front and back of love, I can only attest that I carry the magnificent imprint of what I am and of what I will be. Echoes, resonances, memories, all enlarge me to twice my size and double me again, all with the speed of lightning.

⋆　⋆　⋆

The older I got, the more I walked the streets.

Along with the rest of the shadowy herd, I played a walk-on role on the sidewalk. I sank deeper into the role each day. I sank, I buried myself. I walked under pressure, I moved along in irremediable madness, I lost my way. I disappeared into the sidewalk. Sidewalks! Sidewalks, as far as the eye can see, the only feature in the landscape. Sidewalks! The absolute catchall. I feel it all down my spine: time is passing, little girl. Soon it will be too late to take wing. The sidewalk, a maximum security prison. Escapes don't happen very often hereabouts. I make an indescribable effort to find a solution; I set my memory and my imagination to bubbling. Anguish seizes me, and the terror of the slaughterhouse. There is such a smell in the air and such an odour of one-way traffic. I know I could walk, sidle, day in and day out, without a single ray of reality piercing this place. Anything that happens on the sidewalk will always be strangely deformed. Sidewalks! Sidewalks! They are a narrow band which undulates with the blackness of steel. I am on the sidewalk; they are in the street.

They call it the King's Highway! The street is their business and only theirs. That is where it all happens, where everything is decided. That's where appearances, processions, miracles, garlands, and orders all take place. The street comprises everything that is in a hurry, everything crowded, shooting off, active, everything that is measured in terms of distance, speed and exact time. The air is made up of oil with two drops of acid and three drops of rain. Grindings, smashups, horns, scrap iron, banging, screeching, tail pipes: I mean the cradle of the patriarchy.

I do not want the sidewalks! I do not want the streets! I want something else, another place which I carry in my heart.

It is a place which I have never seen, a joyous place where the wind has room to blow. It is a place they never showed me, a place they could never show me, perhaps because they never knew a place of that kind existed. But I am certain that it does exist and that there I will find a fulfillment made of tender, loose, and interwoven things. It is a place of trees with drops of light on every branch. It is a place with a river into which leaves are falling. I would hear the bark quivering and the sap rising, which would astonish me and give me new notions of joy and hope, cheerful, brilliant notions.

On the sidewalk, the slogan for the great big cowboys with their lassoes is, Get along! Forward! Forward! One step back, two steps back, just like in the good old days when they did the dance of the Star Fairy. Do you get it? Have you taken it in? Good, then onward! Move! Come out of your melancholy! Nostalgia is not good for your morale. What are you nostalgic about? You're never content, never satisfied with anything. Us, the cowboys, we're working ourselves to death for you. Onward! Move! Beat it! Pay attention to the beat. Listen for once! Can't you hear the whistling of the men whose hearts are in their work? You must be deaf! Move it! Onward! Make a woman of yourself! The great whip whistles through the funeral march. A degrading trot for girls made of tears and women made of blood.

I am not alone on the sidewalk. A multitude crowds around me, a crowd of women, of women bent, young, not so young, already old, who are shuffling their feet. I see the streetwalkers from Eden with the pig slop of Genesis all over their boots; I see the survivors of the shipwrecked Ark still trembling in their wet clothes; I see those who, still dazed after the Fall, stumble in the open air; others who escaped the stake are coughing, spitting flames and belching cinders; others, newly crippled by the wedding night, with bandages on their bodies; others, recently raped, who hide their faces in their handkerchiefs and sob like children.

My heart aches. My eyes ache. Tears come to my eyes. My ears and stomach both hurt. In the name of all women, in my own name! We have not been sent to this world to see such things, to submit to such things. Onward! Move it! Beat it!

I am the latest arrival among the shadowy herd. The cowboys have shoved the others together to make a little place for me at the edge of the circuit. They always put the latest arrivals on the outside so they can keep an eye on them, within range of the biggest lassoes. The women give me a dismal, deathly look, a defeated look that is neither friendly nor full of hatred, but simply mournful. Suddenly, what a miracle, one woman straightens up, transformed. Another one! And another! She is not the same. Unbelievable! What is going on? Her mournful look quickly becomes a glance of admiration; she shines in her orbit, then as quickly looks questioningly around. Can she possibly be looking at me? I look around: the women are gazing at the cowboys and the cowboys are gazing back at them. That's all. Nothing more and nothing less. That's enough; it seems that that's enough and that everything is explained by an exchange of looks between a cowboy and some women. What more did I expect? The world of the sidewalk and the world of the street are centred on this fact. Each time a choke looks at one of the women of the herd, the miracle occurs. Right away, it doesn't take two seconds, the woman's mournful look transforms itself, first to admiration, then to interrogation. It happens to the woman right next to me. The change is a direct effect; first one, then the other – it's a real chain reaction. It seems to me that the ancient vocation, function, or life work of women explains this miracle easily enough. Probably all these women were once sibyls, soothsayers, seers, and visionaries whose arts of divination have been recycled into the service of cowboys, chokes, and company. In the presence of these gentlemen, all the women react spontaneously to the riddle: What does he want? What can I do to please him? What's going on? What have I done? What can I do to make him happy so that he'll like me better? The phenomenon of the riddle seems widely spread throughout the whole shadowy herd. What a comedown!

I do my time on the sidewalk. I walk like a zombie. I look for a clientele. I have to find a client before closing time, before the hour of internment and interruption. I change my dress and fix my hair on the sidewalk, which is thick with sugar-daddies. The guys in the street are being tourists; window-shopping, they slam on the brakes of their big cars only inches from my toes in order to amaze and frighten me. They drive holding the wheel with one hand because, with the other, unrepentant students that they are, they consult the latest book of directions for a quick fuck. I shuffle along. I walk for hours, months, years.

★   ★   ★

Then one day, and it was the most beautiful day in my life, I noticed that away over there, far, far away, there were women walking in a direction different from ours. They moved more slowly, descendants of a past I didn't know. What a shock!

I wanted to join them immediately and question them breathlessly, while pressing myself to them. But that was not an easy task: the cowboys didn't like it if we left our place in the herd, and the women of the herd of shadows also tried to keep me from leaving, saying that I was upsetting the order of things. I persisted, my neck stretched out, never losing sight of the women who were walking over there against the grain. Now and then, they disappeared behind the horizon, a mysterious disappearance, only to reappear a little further along, a little later. That made me shake and wriggle with impatience. Bit by bit, I drew nearer to them. I whittled out my passage, inch by inch. As I passed, I asked the women in the herd if they could by chance identify those women who.... Shh! they went, motioning at the cowboys. When I asked indiscreet and dangerous questions, they were silent and mute. Others, more cynical, answered that I had only to ask the cowboys, who knew everything. I didn't want to go back to the beginning, to the edge of the track, to question the chokes. Finally, by asking ceaseless questions left and right, I managed to amass some interesting information. The women who were not walking in circles were suffering from a peculiar disease, worse than leprosy, worse even than the plagues in the patriarchal texts, which had cost them a great deal. The cowboys had imposed severe medical remedies, involving massive injections of anti-bodies. When I saw what I and the other women looked like, I came to the conclusion that the cowboys had in fact discovered the perfect cure, since we were all anti-bodies from the tips of our toes to the tops of our heads. I continued to crawl along patiently, gaining ground inch by inch, slowly passing among the streetwalkers, who averted their heads if I tried merely to greet them and give them a smile of encouragement. I felt alone, cast out from the shadowy herd. Then all at once, there I was! There I was; I had reached the limit of the sidewalk, the world of my childhood and adolescence.

Across the sidewalk, I saw another road, a road bright with light, a road rich with flowers and fields, a road which led away from the sidewalk in gentle curves. I was overcome. It had been so long since I had seen so many flowers all at once.

The last time had been in Ontario on a farm in the promised land, on the wedding day of my day cousin, my night cousin. That morning, my heart was so constricted, my stomach so in knots, I was so close to being sick that I could not appreciate the countryside, where I had passed the day in order to say farewell to the trees and to our creatures as tall as four barley-corns and as broad as four kernels of oats. The marriage of this cataleptic was more like a funeral. The family from Montreal and the family from Ontario nevertheless found ways to celebrate and to make toasts, while I was crying like a baby. The families attributed my tears to nerves, emotion, and to my being tired from the trip. But my cousin looked at me with a funny, sad expression which had *The End* written over it. The choke in question caressed her shoulder and laughed his head off. He'd ridden around all night the night before with his friends. They'd done a good job of burying his bachelor life. Then my cousin started to cry like a baby too. Our respective fathers, frowning, spoke of hysteria. Our mothers, more timid, whipped out their handkerchiefs, blew on our faces to dry our tears, and put a little powder on our noses and around our eyes. Take a deep breath, they said. Take a deep breath to stifle your sobs and still the fluttering of your heart. It will go away. It will go away. See, you're already better. Take a deep breath. Take a deep breath. Once more. Mummy will take care of you the way she did when you were a little baby, a sweet little thing. Calm yourself, my darling, or daddy will have to send for the doctor, the nasty doctor with his big needles. Take a deep breath and come to mummy's arms.

That was the last time that I was in my mother's arms. That was the last time I saw so much grass, light, birds, and sweet, strong, nourishing beauty. But then I came down to earth again. The promised land was within arm's reach and I was immobilized. Can you believe it? I was immobilized. Immobilized for the first time since when? No, I could not tell, since it was lost in the night-time of my last paralyis. I was no longer quickstepping along the sidewalk, exhausted, empty and desperate, and, when I opened my eyes, the same limited horizon closing in, and the strangling lassoes, and all around me, the crippled, the burnt, the drowned, the martyred women, and the former sibyls bemused by riddles.

I was in the process of incarnating myself.

Such a blossoming sensation in my tree-body, in the branches of  my arms, the roots of my legs, the flowers of my fingers, the leaves of my hair, the dewdrops of my mouth, and the stars of my imagination! I was born. The divine infant was born, for herself alone. My joints sprang to life and I frisked about. I met women to whom the same thing was happening. I became happy, even mad with joy. I ripened, my skin was warm, I began to move, I greeted other women who greeted me in turn, who smiled, who stopped for a little chat – when I had been on the sidewalk, I had never imagined that there were so many of them. It may be a question of recognition: the more you deny someone, the more she disappears and then becomes invisible; but only one or two drops of recognition will revive the dead body.

I stayed there for a very long time. The women gave me sanctuary and nourishment as though I was their equal. I read, like a starving person, all the books they lent me. I discovered the world and I reconciled myself with language, painting, and sculpture. I digested everything; I assimilated it all. I had wasted a considerable amount of time on the sidewalk.... It took me an incredible amount of time merely to recognize my own hand stretched out in front of me. It took another incredibly long time merely to comprehend that I could speak, draw, and move my body and my limbs all by myself, as I needed and wanted to. And it took me years to finally understand, once and for all, that I did not have to have plague or leprosy in order to live here in no-man's-land.

Now and then, as infrequently as possible, I returned to those who were still on the sidewalk. My childhood friends were there. My mother was there. I wanted so much to share my new learning with them. I knew that I was running risks, and that the chokes were on the watch everywhere, their fangs bared, their flick-knives poised over my tongue. They did not listen to me; they wanted to hear nothing at all. My friends, my sisters, all averted their heads. If I came too near them, they pushed me away with angry, even disgusted gestures. But most of all, they were afraid! They made threats, they warned me, they made pessimistic predictions, while all the time continuing to march backward.

I spaced out my visits and contented myself with calling them on the phone now and then, because I was loyal and because I had a sense of continuity. And I called because I was sad and because their rejection of me plunged my heart into grief. I called. I phoned frequently from afar, from my long distance. It became difficult, complicated, and frustrating to phone the herd of shadows. The telephone, the whole vast communications network, belongs, as I am sure you know, to the stranglers with the big lassoes – the term "communication," which they use so lightly, refers to a very different notion from mine. I have noticed that they communicate most often through violence, despair, dead ends, contempt, and indiscretion.

Perhaps I'm prejudiced. If this is how I react, it comes about because they make me live through the same four scenarios each time I try to get in touch with the women. The first scenario: I dial the number; the line is always busy. The second scenario: I dial the number; it rings, but no one answers. Third scenario: I dial the number; it rings;

someone picks up the receiver, but no one speaks to me. Fourth scenario: I dial the number; it rings; someone picks up the phone and, before I get in a single word, dumps all over me. The telephone is just like the patriarchy!

I've had it. I've given up. I don't call anymore and I don't play missionary sister. After all, the desire to live, to grow, the fury of hope – these I cannot get across on the telephone.

Yesterday I was seated at the foot of the tree called Mother-in-flower in the living night of my new land. I was there with all my happiness, with all the intimate movements of my veins and arteries and of my imagination. In the silence of the constellations, I saw the Moon rise in the sky, blood of my blood, strength of my strength, hope of my hope, reliquary of my time of childhood in the land of America. Later, a woman came. She kissed me. I kissed her. I gazed at her.

For the first time in my life, I had just eaten, I had just drunk, without a thought for death.

Winter 1978-Spring 1979
Montréal
Rivière Ouareau

for Gloria Orenstein

NIGHT COWS

MY MOTHER IS A COW! That makes two of us.

Two beautiful milk cows, butter cows; creators of those sweet oceans of magnetic milk which surge through the human body. Two beautiful brown beasts, as the saying goes. All cows, regardless of race, weight, or colour, are castrated young. Why, you ask? Because, with certain rare exceptions, the beautiful brown beasts are nymphomaniacs. The ancestral defect is in my mother as it is in all of us, no matter how much holy water or dishwater she drinks.

Cows are at the bottom rung of the ladder of infinity. Damned cows!

Sometimes they were castrated for moral reasons, sometimes for financial reasons. The monetary advantages of castration are undeniable because, it seems, this is the best method of maximizing the profits to the butcher from cows whose value is noticeably reduced by their pathological condition. Throughout the centuries, the operators of the Order of Castrators have recognized to a man that a castrated cow behaves herself more dependably, more normally, than a cow who is intact. Not to mention that her moral attitudes are directed more forcefully toward the nutritive principle. Oh, yes. No more of the so-called milk from nymphomaniac cows – all curdled, with no butter fat! No more of the putrid so-called milk that tastes of rotten clay and oily water. Forget that milk that turns red from its scandalous blood-secret. Castration is really a kind of blessing for these day cows, these cows of good will. This discovery of the miracle of mutilation transforms a nymphomaniac cow into a beast which can be specialized to produce meat, milk, butter, and labour.

My mother is a cow, of an abundant breed. My mother is an income-producing animal, a fixed asset which it is in the interests of the owners to maintain as long as her regularity lasts.

By day, my mother's general outline comprises all female forms. A well-made cow, my mother has broad haunches, abundant mammary secretions, high buttocks, wide pelvis, deep chest and broad hips. Altogether her body is long and well padded. Her eye is limpid and sweet, sweet, sweet; her head is yielding and her ears small. In short, she has everything which indicates a tranquil and submissive nature. It is also fundamental that she walks on all fours.

By day, I see her wandering aimlessly, sweating, slobbering, and swelling. She sniffs everywhere, breathing everything in — even in the bottoms of beds or of pockets, for letters in the mail, sniffing out, I believe, omens of her impending disappearance. By day, you could say that my mother is made of a mud that will not hold its shape, of clay that would crack in the oven. But the moment night approaches, with its waterfalls of dreams, and the birds of the earth mount the wind of the branches, I see my mother transform herself. She transforms herself fleetingly, from the outside. She transforms herself smoothly, from the inside.

I, the heifer, the little cow, have observed my mother for so long a time that I can tell you at what precise moment the happy metamorphosis of a day cow to a cow of the night begins. It begins at sunset when the evening song starts floating freely through the old kitchens of our houses. Everybody to bed! Everyone is asleep. Then my mother begins by bathing her body, the vast expanse of her body, in the heavenly water. This is the first step by which she will presently emerge magnificent.

By day, my mother appears shabby, even drab, but at night she takes out her black and white gown, the one that has spots scattered here and there, their flickering producing an extraordinary suggestion of midnight blue. And that gown, I must tell you, has a splendour of its own. It seems to have swallowed up the starry sky on a night when the moon is full. And that gown clings to her body from neck to foot. My mother is so beautiful! A beauty. Her fine, supple, living skin, covered with short and shining hair, her milky teats, her belly where the fur lies in sweet and lustrous waves, her horns, which she flattens out by day, tucking them discreetly under her chignon, but which she wears at night like the crescent moon, with their points thrusting forward. A beauty, my mother, a beauty perpetually tempered by the drops of milk which fall noiselessly in our solitude.

When she invests me, in my turn, in my night dress, a double enchantment binds us to one another. My most beautiful dress, far more beautiful than my Sunday clothes; a dress which varies in colour from palest red to the red of blood buried in the depths of the heart. At the top of my dress, near the flanks, there is another shade of red, the kind of red seen on the backs of trout which dart like threads in the shadowy bottoms beneath the icy waters of the rivers of our north. It's strange, strange, but each time my mother drapes me once more in my red gown, I feel she has given birth to me anew.

And we are off! We are going elsewhere, jubilation for our bodies, food for our hunger, air for our lungs and veins; we are going elsewhere toward our night of the fleshy cows. And we mount higher and higher through the cycles of the heavens. Next to each other, turning toward each other, bearing the scars of our mutilation, sharing the desire to travel together out of the depths of the time we serve by day in the old kitchens. This exploding desire cannot be conquered and expands our sweet orifices. Cradled in ecstasies! The millennial swing which sweeps us out of the daily eclipse of the slaughterhouse. There we are, all naked within our garments, within the flesh of our garments of night, within the embrace of the hairs of our skin. Daughter, mother, mother, daughter, the hierarchy goes off to take a holiday when the cows of the night bathe themselves in the lakes of sweaty tenderness.

And we are off! And we fly to our rendezvous in the Milky Way. How beautiful! The great river of milk, the land of birth, where mothers and daughters are reunited at long last. So beautiful! Canals of milk blooming with water lilies. Milk-drunk, white flow, fluid star, the fruit of our mother's guts expands across the brisk climate of the sky. All the breasted creatures of the universe come to the meeting place. Light-footed they come, laughing in the gorgeous milk-dawn which flows from the cows of the night. Mad dashes down the curve of the spine, misty hooves of comet-mammals. All breasted creatures are uniting with each other in a wave of scales, of hair, of tenderness.

The milk flows! The milk spurts! The milk comes in floods! Beautiful, beautiful bovine bounty. A snowstorm of milk! Gulps of milk!

Scents of milk! Drifts of milk! Gusts of milk! Hurricanes of milk! Clouds of milk! Milk clotted with images! Rainbows of milk! Milk erupts from bursting females, from breasts which make nourishment from the throbbing of life. And from all sides arise rallying cries, a tumult of emotions stimulated by the milk. The daughters' implacable thirst demands the milk lap through the heavenly shallows; it demands the milk not clot in the teats nor run off down the steep sides of the void. I know and will say it. The living world does not derive from dream! The living world does not arise from wrath! The living world springs from the mothers' mammalian brains. Oh yes, oh yes! Their white brain matter is yet another glorious milk which starts to flow in times of celebration.

And we are there! We emerge, panting, from the full-blowing wind. And they are there, they are all there, those tempestuous breasted creatures: those with hooves and those with nails; those with claws, with webbed feet, and with greedy, churning, milky, buttery mouths. They come on two feet and on four, the terrestrial motors of their hearts are swelling the white cantata of the milky way. They come, the mammals mistaken for fish because they swim. And the mammals mistaken for birds because they fly on wings of skin. Horns, antlers, claws, and scales, each is gorgeously bedecked, here where the passionate questions fall like bursting grapes. Animal emanations, a definitive perfume to be bottled in memory,. These arise from that great intimate desire which distends their membranes, stretches the tips of their antlers to the point where they take off into female identity, into the recognition of blood, roots, excess, and passion!

Milk is running! A flood tide of milk.

Here is a holiday of hooves in the milky way. The hooves of those cursed cows of the night make the roof of heaven vibrate.

My mother is a cow! That makes two of us. Oh, how happy my mother is at this moment. What hope dawns in her imagination? What moist resonance, grainy with salt and sound, slides down the back of her tongue? My mother is filled to bursting, she expands, she beds herself down in the estuaries of her body. My mother is larger than giants, larger than underground cities, larger than those sheets of water which mix with the salt sea in the ocean gulfs. My mother is happy. I can see, I can taste her happiness as she starts to secrete her beautiful milk through the roots of the hair of her black and white gown. I slide toward the perfumed flavour which wells up from her body. Oh, the hot odour of foaming nectar at the fringe of her forest of fur, at the break of a particular light which streams toward my mouth. I drink, I suckle. My thirst is a conduit for my mother's strength, for immortal desire, for the white bounty in the life of my body. The milk dribbles from my lips. I am distended. Now she envelops me in her skin which she has unfolded. A wool rug, my mother ripples through the length of her skin, and I can see through her body because her flesh has almost the transparence of crystal polished by fire. My mother opens herself in two, she splits herself in four, so that I may reunite with her, so that I may find her again in her own substance and in the coursing currents of her night dress.

Oh, the beautiful fabric absorbed in the fullness of its fibres, of its network of nerves, its green foam, its salty sponges. Oh, the foliage of its internal stars where the tangles of slaked thirst, of satisfied hunger are centred. I visit my breast mother, my fruit-mother, my plant-mother, my scaly, visceral mother in the heat of her blood, the geology of her layers of skin. I view her soul, her vulva, her womb, her rosy nectar, the mineral illuminations of her grottoes. I taste it all. Near the elevations of her throat, a weeping willow sheds its tears of sap. My night cow swallows me, digests me as if I were a weed or half-ripe fruit, and I glow, I touch her everywhere.

My mother gives a leap! I know we are leaving once more and I anchor myself in the river which flows around her heart. My mother is galloping. We are going further. She speeds up to the same beat as the wings of the thunderbird. We are leaving again, and I stick my head out to look around. We are galloping toward the northern tundra, where the body of North America ends in a bleached and pallid gesture. We are galloping toward the tundra, and my mother's hooves leave in their track a trail of stars. I leap on my mother's back. She is galloping. We are vaulting through caverns of air. The whole flock of breasted creatures is leaving. We are going to the tundra to wake the crows.

How beautiful! The birds of calamity are asleep in their dormitories. How beautiful! Touch not the crows with your dead man's hands; don't interfere with these women who aspire only to fly. How beautiful! The sly and distrustful ones sleep in their nests in spirals under the snowy clumps of fir trees. Notice the colour of the crows — part black dirt and part blood from the shafts of their feathers. The crows sleep only in the warmth of their own wings and surrounded by sentinels. The birds of calamity remember the crows crucified on the doors of barns. They remember the shot in the wing and the interminable fall into death. They remember the feet cut by the blade in the traps. They remember the terrible poison hidden in the baits spread out for a feast.

Tell me, mother, why are the crows so black? Because, my child, the night of the doves has fallen on their feathers.

And we are going to wake the crows! Northward to snow's end, then southward to where they flock in their millions in the rookeries of the open sky. We find our way south by following the belt of corn. A-gallop, a-gallop! They welcome us, instantly bracing themselves on the fresh night air. Once more we raise the incantation of flight, and the whole American continent, from north to south, is lovely in the beauty of the flesh and feathers which fly over it. It is a celebration for the sister crows and the mammals; a time of rediscovered joys, of all possible embraces in body and in memory. All is made visible in a dazzling conjunction of feathers, scales, and cries. The crows' little beaks give great big kisses, the mammals' great mouths make huge lapping kisses, there is a grasping of small hands and embracing in the sweet land of hair, of sensory silks. Each touches the other's splendid garments, her rosy openings, her female roundness moist with dew. Each feels the pulse of the other, each feels the other's tenderness and her firm-fixed desire to welcome. From mouth to mouth, how can I express it! What can I say of the arousals, the endearments? They touch. They nuzzle. They lick. The devil is in the cows!

And later, but only after this sweet dance of recognition, the crows light their corncob pipes. This is the long-awaited moment! The crows light their corncob pipes, puffing deeply while ruffling their feathers, and start to relate, to recount in every way, to skim the radiant surface of everything they remember regarding us. In their bird brains they seem to have some recollection of everything. Only among them can we learn to remember. What they recount to us is

78

troubling. What they are saying is terrible! Every night when they open their beaks, it is as if a kiss of fire empties itself down our throats. Every night the crows tell us the same story, and every time the tale grows richer because they continually add to it further detail and a new clarity. When, between two puffs of tobacco, they start to relate the appearance of the first mammalian brain on earth, it is easy to believe, in the silence which reigns, that we hear the first drop of milk falling on the promised land.

The crows give us back our female history before the establishment of the Order of Castrators. It is staggering to hear described out loud the texture of the lives of our ancestral mothers, those mammals of the heights and the depths, to hear about those beasts who reaped and were gentle, rapturous, and kind; who held their children's hands the night through; to know their ardour, their dreams, their affections, their long promenades by wellsprings of islands, and their mutual discoveries which flourished like an appletree in bloom on the verge of summer. What the crows say moves us. What the crows say gradually becomes ominous as though a time of mourning must always follow a time of joy.

The story of what followed the Mother Age speaks only of exterminations, massacres, extortion, the long march of the females to the slaughterhouse, to the stake, the mass grave, the bridal suites of torture. Nothing relieves the account of rapes and murders, of knives drawn in vengeance across miserable throats. Now, in this uncertain light, it is all said; it all has to be said. The smoke rises, the crows light another corncob pipe and recount it all again. Every night, someone rises, while her sister crows tamp their pipes. Someone rises in her turn to relate what she remembers. Sometimes it is a whale who speaks of extermination. Sometimes a bison who speaks of massacre and slaughter. Or a ewe-lamb, who speaks of sacrifice. Or a jenny-ass to tell of the pitchfork in her belly. Or a she-bear, a baby mammoth, or a bat, all speaking their fury, their rage. They speak it, they yelp it, they bay it, they croak it, they screech it, they weep it, they sing it, so that finally the Age of Females will have more substance than a wisp of fog or a moment of silence in their memories. Even the most cursed of all these cursed females rises bit by bit out of her former vagueness and nonexistence.

How quickly time passes as we listen to each heart speaking in the Milky Way. Suddenly we realize that the sun threatens to rise and the men down below threaten to investigate the joyous noise they heard all night above their heads. We leave in a final gallop, seeing the crows back to their dormitories, and each of us heads back to her perch, her old kitchen, her pool of mud, her sliver of space. Farewell! But only for now, my sisters. Indeed, we will see one another again!

Because every night, each cow of night loves herself so well and hopes so hard, and teaches herself so much consciousness and pride, that I know we approach the moment when we will redeem the promised land, and then, oh then, in one rush of recognition, in one cry of passion, we will call it by a new and better name.

Winter 1979
Montréal

for Martine Landriault

THE
ANGEL MAKERS

(Translator's Note: "Faiseuse d'ange" *is a Québec expression denoting women who perform illegal abortions.)*

I TELL A TALE.

In the sweet spring air, the birds are singing — now is the time to pick flowers, to brush the rivers with your eyes, to immerse yourself bird-fashion in the wash of delight.

My mother is knitting. See how the soft yarn foams in her basket. My mother always knits with wool which was washed on the backs of the living beasts, and an entire valley is displayed in her basket when she fondles the yarns to bring them nearer her hands.

At once, the wool of the whole flock springs into motion and I hear the drumming of hooves, the panting of souls, the births of the fleeces travelling along the strands like the thoughts my mother might think for herself, for me.

In her basket, I recognize the wool of a ewe-lamb and that of a she-camel. There is also the hair of a reindeer in her northern coat and some from a rabbit who paused in her bounding rush. In her basket I hear the clatter of falling rocks. It comes from the wool of a Peruvian goat who is greeting a goat from the Himalayas and one from the Rocky Mountains with her great mammalian gaze.

Knit one! Purl one! My mother starts her knitting with puffy yarn and thick needles. She is able to knit cardigans, dresses and suits, but she knits nothing but scarves.

In red! She knits in red! A magnetic, frenetic, pulsating red! A biographical red which is definitively triumphant over all that is neutral, objective, void, and neat. And, I don't know why, her scarf always ends up looking like an Amazon banner.

At home, the time devoted to my mother's knitting is sacred. It is a reassuring moment for some, even though others are uneasy, are anxious.

In the midst of all the mistrust, rumour, spying, I feel a universal tempest in my mother's wools. Each of her stitches, and the one following, and the one following that, and the one after that, is like a cell filled with air, a fabled vortex, an extended holding of the breath. I have never heard anything which spoke as clearly as my mother's knitting needles.

Knit one, purl one. Open up your eyes and ears, exist in the openings of your body and your heart if you want to see my mother's famous pattern stitch. See and hear her famous alternating *needle-thrust* from the beginning, made of the pure tide of the Flood. See and hear her *rice thrust,* an open *thrust* which feeds the imaginary, which keeps the wool from withering away before its metamorphosis. And her French *border-thrust* which edges the banner, her English *slip-thrust,* her American *cross-thrust,* her *queen-mother-thrust,* her *sovereign-thrust.*

Purl one, purl two, see how she thrusts the left-hand needle, how she lets slip the yarn which runs from the ball across the stitch and lets it fall. My mother is preparing the angel-stitch!

★   ★   ★

It grows chilly. Crows are calling — the millennia roll through their calls, and when the body's memory is caught by their cries, we might believe they foretell the future.

My mother is a legend!

She relates to the dead, to that condition which is painful and full of uncertainty. I myself affirm that my mother exists and that I exist intermingled with her, with her characteristics, with her flesh, within her joints, within whatever has penetrated to her bones.

My mother exists.

She puts on her coat, her running shoes, her scarf, arranges her needles, the thick ones and the graduated ones and the circular ones, in her basket, along with her bobbins. Basket on her arm, she steps outside. The emptiness of the street vibrates when it sees the red scarf wrapped around my mother's neck.

My mother exists and that fact makes me ecstatic.

She is a knitter. She wields a knife! Once, sometimes twice a week she goes somewhere else to knit. The best knitter in the parish, no one can beat her at it.

She proceeds down the street just like a heroine, enveloped in clouds and mist which hide her from the eyes of the police and from whoever is on their side. When she leaves, I become gently accustomed to her absence. But I am afraid. I am afraid! Supposing she doesn't come back. They might punish her; they might kill her!

My mother is not within her rights; she is not part of the legality of handcuffs or of legitimate punishment. "Raise your right hand and swear." If you believe that my mother will agree to perjure herself by taking that old primitive oath on the father's testicles, right hand outstretched, fingers spread, and in her eyes the ancient terror of the animal caught in a trap, then you don't have a heart. My mother will never extend anything but her left hand filled with promise and with the fruit of entrails together with their children molded in the interior of the red pulp.

Rights, right-thinking, the right side, my mother knows that the right makes up the most unfeeling part of the body, the part that can only express what is human by mixing it up with the sternest law in the most horrible way. Their rights, the right side, belong to the part of the body which least remembers its sojourn in the mother's belly, the immense tenderness of our origins. Those rights are the rights to contempt, to amnesia. The goal: to eliminate that most annoying memory of the mother's participation in the birth of children, wherever something of it might remain in the depth of the senses or in the first stirrings of passion. The right, the power, to spit where you want, the tacit authorization, the rights of the blood, the deaths of the mothers in labour, the right of the first night, the sperm-saturated rape. All rights of reproduction are reserved to the editor; the birthright is for men only; the right to go in and out, that fundamental right of man, spatial right; the right hand of the father is the seat of the just; a notion which is the foundation for the geometry of murderers.

The natural position, the true position of the foetus in the mother's belly, is a left-turning position. As in the southern heights above the mother mountains, the greatest constellation of the heavens, and its outline of fate.

Their rights, the right way, are the part of the body which throws back its head in refusal. The intrauterine position of the foetus is to the left! But let's forget that immediately and right the barrier, quickly, right away!

My mother decidedly did not get off on the right foot when she left her mother's belly. Too bad for her if she is out of line, troublesome, deviant, uncomfortable, awkward. Since she is left-handed, she risks being caught as she makes the angel-stitch on her thick needles.

★   ★   ★

It is now glacially cold. Having received an anonymous accusation, they set out in pursuit of her with a roar. Their electric wail stirs a paralyzing primeval fear. Car Zero, calling Zero. Attention! Attention! All patrols on alert. Do you read me? But where has that twisted pervert, that murderess gone? Car Zero, calling Zero. Do you read me? Where is the angel maker hiding? The patrol cars cruise the streets, brutally illuminating the dark corners of doorways with their revolving lights. Their strident electric wail recalls the old days when the mob sneered and sniggered as mothers in chains were hurled into the pit or burned at the stake. Car Zero, calling Zero. The sirens swell and suffocate. It is glacially cold.

It's gotten hot: a natural warmth transmitted intact to the warm tears in the phosphorescent sea.

In the safety of the room, my mother knits the angel-stitch, the warm stitch of a mother's rage, of the rage of the entire female race. The more she knits, the further the walls withdraw, withdraw about the darkening country where the sirens wail.

Tonight there are errors and misses in their barrage, in the line they trace.

As my mother knits, she bows lower and lower. As she knits, my mother is bent over because everything rests on her back – their laws, Noah's Ark, the Old and the New Testaments, that ignoble inheritance, that voracious teeming of generations which has been fused from women's bellies. See what she supports on her back as she bends over the mother's belly, parting the white waves of the sheets, parting the legs.

Whispers of blood, cataracts of water. A kiss of silt and of red clay. The woman's body is stretched, split, it foams, it is reanimated when what was enfolded in her spreads its wings. The angel leaves the deep heaven of the body, gliding down softly, sweetly, just like a stork's descent on the promised land. All growth interrupted, the angel is translucent in her diaphanous shroud. Light as a feather! The angel has no shadow, no name, no father.

In the room, the two women hold each other by the hand. They look at each other, laughing, crying, expressing every shade of emotion.

Whispers of blood: my mother says that they are not killers. They have merely slowed the panicky course of the hypnotized toward the most negative level of life. They have merely interrupted the cycle of reincarnation, since at birth the newborn already bears the names of its ancestors, of its grandparents, uncles, of saints and heroes. My mother says they have halted succession, lunacy, family, waste, and gangrene. By risking their lives, they have tried to exhaust the shopkeeper's inventory.

The angel makers, witches, hysterical women, the bad fucks, old cows, bitches in heat, wild cats, old mares, birds of ill omen, non-virgins, whores, lesbians, unnatural mothers, loose women, crazy ladies, chattering magpies, cock-teasers, the depressed and the sluts, like those two there, have already been burnt, and they will be hanged on top of that.

There is singing in the kitchen. My mother sets the table, preparing a feast for the weakened convalescent, who stretches an accustomed hand toward the stove and pots. They are both humming as the vegetables go into the kettle.

My mother stirs up the fire and the odours explode. In the pot, the smallest, most succinct of herbs unfold their petals. Cabbage leaves, chives, onions, carrots, celery, diced turnip, barley and slightly crunchy rice, bones and their marrow, all dance and sing together, a mellow juice like liquid stars. The chives are like seaweed, the carrots have the outline of horns, the cabbage leaves are the petals of a volcanic flower, a rib of celery cuts the soup like a dorsal fin, the tomatoes get under way all of a sudden, insinuating their red and green sparks among the white onions.

Side by side, thigh to thigh, loving, famished, they devour the soup the way a fire consumes. They revive. My mother picks up her knitting, wakes up the beasts in her basket and tugs lightly at her yarns. The ewe-lamb gives a furtive bleat. The beasts with manes, strong, insistent, hold their tongues. My mother untangles her yarns. The two women rock. Two women and the beasts rock, talk together, listen to one another, knit a future for themselves, unravelling analogies of life and then of death. The setting forth, which is shared with no one; motherhood, the fulfilled universe which wants to fulfill itself again.

They have lighted the lamps which are only lit at night in the houses.

They help each other; they teach each other things. They help each other climb with a she-wolf's step right to the heart, so that hope may rise again. The invitation to the feast. They rock, they speak to one another, they acknowledge each other, and, little by little, their rocking turns into the footsteps of a giantess.

The air is sweet ... in all its splendour, an angel passes!

Spring 1979, Rivière Ouareau

POSTFACE

by Gloria Feman Orenstein

FOR THE FIRST time in its long history from Sappho to Adrienne Rich, from Renée Vivien to Rita Mae Brown, an extraterrestrial heroine makes her appearance in lesbian literature, heralding the advent of a new myth of origins for woman-identified women.

The Lesbianchild protagonist of Jovette Marchessault's "A Lesbian Chronicle from Medieval Quebec" lives out all the archetypal motifs of the classic myth of the birth of the hero, in terms that prefigure her identity as a potential leader or saviour of her people. However, the way in which she breaks with all the patriarchal premises of that mythic model transforms the meaning of heroism for women today.

Traditionally, male mythic heroes of a particular national or spiritual vision, such as Jesus, Sargon, Moses, Oedipus or Perseus, have been described as being of divine, spiritual, or noble origin. Often they were abandoned by their parents in order to escape infanticide or because an oracle predicted that their birth would bring about evil or destruction. They were frequently raised in exile by people of humble stock who were totally unaware of the child's true identity. This invisibility throughout their early childhood and adolescence is eventually terminated by events which lead them to answer the call of their heroic destiny.

Marchessault's autobiographical Lesbianchild-Self is marked for a similar heroic apotheosis through the mythic implications of the ritual passages in her life cycle. Like many traditional mythic heroes, she, too, is of extraterrestrial origin and is raised humbly and invisibly among the common people. She is also exiled in a foreign land – a land colonized by alien patriarchal oppressors. Her identity as daughter of the Mother Goddess, child of the race of inhabitants of the lost continent of Atlantis, is unknown to those who govern the country in which she resides. Moreover, all memory of such a powerful gynocentric heritage has been wiped out through centuries of massacre, censorship and taboo.

Here at last is the modern mythic image of the Lesbian as the prophet of a new cycle of history and as the creator of a new interpretation of time, space, and being. Her emergence into consciousness announces the coming of a revolutionary feminist era that will put an end to the accumulated karma of destruction, revenge and tyranny that has always characterized patriarchal heroism. Marchessault, however, makes important reversals in the male mythic pattern by indicting God the Father and having the heroine choose to define her existence independently of men and of all male ideology. Her heroic power derives from her affirmation of the joys of womanloving love and from her reverence for the potent natural energies of the earth.

The "Lesbian Chronicle" tells us that in medieval Quebec (a city of the psychic interior, as well as a contemporary politico-religious reality locatable anywhere on the Judeo-Christian map), the daughters of a lost Lesbian Nation, the descendants of a forgotten female divinity, are reclaiming their primordial matristic heritage. As womanheroes, they are responding to the same mythic call to a sacred mission that the great heroes of all time have always answered – the call to justice, to freedom, and to spiritual autonomy. By repossessing their ancient reverence for a Mother Goddess, they are asserting the original fecundity, energy and creative potential that naturally and legitimately reside within all women.

In renouncing her subscription to the telephonic dis/connection at the conclusion of the "Chronicle," the new lesbian feminist heroine plugs out patriarchy and tunes in to the higher spiritual call of her lost, female Ancestors. She sensitizes her entire being to their haunting cries – to the buried voices from the past of wise womanloving women, burned as heretics and witches because of their knowledge of the earth's healing forces and because of their love for each other. Lesbianism, in Marchessault's vision, is not merely defined in terms of female sexuality. It is a total world view, an identity of an entire people whose desires and creations have been erased from the record of human history. Lesbian love, as Marchessault envisages it, signifies existence outside of the Death Culture. In Lesbian Culture all of the dimensions of life are eroticized. Thus, a link is established between Lesbianism and a life-giving, ecstatic, gynergic cultural ethos.

The first lesbian embrace, this "Kiss of Life" narrated in the "Chronicle," prefigures the heroine's rebirth into what radical feminist theologian Mary Daly has called a "metapatriarchal," self-transforming journey towards a gyn-ecological consciousness, one that affirms that everything in the universe is connected in one all-embracing totality. Calling for an exorcism of the "mind/spirit/body pollution inflicted through patriarchal myth and language on all levels,"[1] Daly states that "Gyn/Ecology is by and about women a-mazing all the male-authored 'sciences of womankind,' and weaving world tapestries *of our own kind.* That is, it is about dis-covering, de-veloping the complex web of living/loving relationships *of our own kind.* It is about women living, loving, creating our Selves, our cosmos. It *is* dis-possessing our Selves, enspiriting our Selves, hearing the call of the wild, naming our wisdom, spinning and weaving world tapestries out of genesis and demise."[2]

"A Lesbian Chronicle from Medieval Quebec" dramatizes the cosmic dimensions of a war between two worlds locked in fatal battle, the clash between a violent, destructive culture and a gyn-ecological vision. Annihilating the phallocratic death demons of Christianity through an initial cycle of exorcism, the "Chronicle" posits a new spiritual world view in which female desire is redeemed in an expanded lunar space-time cycle of jubilation.

This cultural conflict is a mythic recapitulation of actual prehistory as it is now being revealed to us by archaeologists such as Marija Gimbutas.[3] Marchessault's mythic imagination succeeds in intuiting facts now borne out by studies of matristic cultures of Old Europe dating from the Upper Paleolithic to the Bronze Age, which attest to the conquering of goddess-worshipping, women-centred cultures by Indo-European hordes who brought patriarchal rule, a father-god, and war to preexisting matristic societies.

Excavations from Čatal Huyuk (6500-5500 BCE) in Anatolia and from Crete reveal that the Goddess was symbolized by a Mother and Daughter pair just as Marchessault depicts her in "Night Cows." In Crete the Goddess was also imaged as a horned cow with her calf.

The legendary Amazons from the second and first millennia were hybrids of both the Old European matristic cultures and the patriarchal Indo-Europeans. They appear to have reacted strongly against the advent of the patristic system and its accompanying violent destruction of the age of the Religion of the Great Mother. Marchessault's Lesbianchild, like the Amazons of old, rebels against a similar patriarchal oppression. In "Night Cows" Mother and Daughter reenact the reclamation of the knowledge of their true identity as sacred epiphanies of the Great Goddess incarnated in the images of Mother Cow and Daughter Calf.

There is an astonishing visionary accuracy in the mythic pattern cast for us by the author of these three texts. The contrast between the Day Cows and the Night Cows comes to represent symbolically the fundamental opposition between patristic and matristic visions of the female.

In contrast with the large body of lesbian literature of the past that has portrayed the lesbian as a victim, as a potential madwoman or suicide, whose secret love life had to remain hidden and whose identity had to be made permanently invisible in order to ensure survival, and in rejection of all previous stereotypes of lesbians as masculine women, neurotic women, tainted women, or exalted women, escaping from political and sexist realities to an idyll of lovemaking on the Isle of Lesbos, Marchessault's Lesbianchild is a proud woman warrior and an "enfant terrible." She is, above all, a survivor and a creator, who dares to become visible, to break the terrible silence, to blaspheme and to mock the sadistic ceremonies of Christianity that constantly violate the female mind and spirit.

This daughter of the race of Amazons delves into her vast memory of desire to recall the ancient lost matristic paradise when love between women prevailed, the time before the coming of the Order of Castrators that Marchessault speaks of in "Night Cows." The Lesbianchild's psyche has preserved intact the dream of prepatriarchal days when the female imagination was free to invent a space-time of exaltation and tenderness.

As the Lesbianchild reaches adolescence in the Land of Permanent Sacrifice, the theme of the betrayal of women by men, and by their sisters who have been conditioned by male ideology, emerges as the ultimate sin of patriarchy. The "Chronicle" is not only a record of mind-rape and body-rape, it is also the story of this vaster betrayal. Abandoned by her female cousin in favour of a male suitor, the Lesbian adolescent suffers the consummate pain of a woman raised in a male-worshipping society – the pain of losing womanlove.

However, the Lesbian's final withdrawal from communication with patriarchal structures does not arise from an a priori anti-male bias. It is not so much a withdrawal of energy as a returning of female energy to women. It arises from the self-defining, self-affirming strength that is released in her gynergic centre, as her consciousness is awakened to the nature of female experience in an androcentric universe. Adrienne Rich, in a text entitled "The Meaning of Our Love For Women Is What We Have Constantly to Expand," has explained the difference very clearly.

> When we are totally, passionately engaged in working and acting and communicating with and for women, the notion of 'withdrawing energy from men' becomes irrelevant: we are already cycling our energy among ourselves. We must remember that we have been penalized, vilified, and mocked, not for hating men, but for loving women. The meaning of our love for women is what we have constantly to expand. [4]

All of Jovette Marchessault's creative work in literature and the visual arts is a celebration of that cycling of female energy that Adrienne Rich describes.

In Marchessault's mythico-poetic universe, the figures of the Lesbianchild and the Mother transform the traditional Mother-Daughter archetype into a compelling new image of ecstatic sisterhood. They represent the two basic feminist principles of spiritual revolution and rebirth. Both Mother and Daughter are Lesbians in the sense that Marchessault defines Lesbianism, for they only come to life and relate to each other in a passionate new dynamic outside of the patriarchal Death Culture. It is the figure of the mother that links the two accompanying texts "Night Cows" and "The Angel Makers" to the "Chronicle," creating a Mother-Daughter triptych, in which the Lesbianchild becomes a unique symbol for spiritual motherhood in a feminist world – a view that conceives of Birth as a transformatory process that takes place in the realm of the creative imagination. In Marchessault's works, the figure of the Mother is always multidimensional. Mothers are at once mammalian and human, mythic and real, celestial and terrestrial. Her constellation of the archetypes in the female psyche and her interpretation of the reality of female experience coincide in portraying Mothers as Wise Women, Seekers, Healers, and Creators. They are the spirit guides who give birth to new knowledge, new perceptions, new relationships, new works, and a new reality.

In "Night Cows," Cow-Mother, who is both Mother-Goddess and Mother-Parent, embarks upon the ultimate female vision-quest journey to seek the truth about the origins and overthrow of female power. She ritually initiates her Lesbian daughter to the female mysteries of the body and the spirit, mothering and nurturing her with desire in ways that are forbidden under patriarchy. The new Mother-Daughter relationship depicted in "Night Cows" is one of hope, exaltation and celebration.

Whether as mythic mammalian Cow-Mother or as an Angel Maker, the Mother is always related to the archetype of the Great Mother Goddess, as a weaver and spinner of a heroic new destiny for women. Abortion is envisaged as a high form of spiritual rebirth in a world where maternity leads to victimization. The Angel Maker is thus transformed into the revolutionary new image of the spiritual midwife, assisting women in giving birth to their new identities as autonomous, liberated women, who consciously make a choice in favour of personal freedom and planetary survival. This text reverses the meaning of the Annunciation for women, for the coming of the Angel in the role of an Angel Maker no longer announces an inevitable and unexpected birth. Instead her manifestation heralds a time in which women will bestow upon each other the gift of freedom from the future burden of all such births. The Angel Maker is a modern alchemist and a spirit healer. She is your mother, my mother, a guardian angel, and the mother of a new race of women who, like the Lesbianchild of the "Chronicle," will give birth to the creative giants buried deep within themselves.

This collection of Mother-Daughter texts can be understood as a cycle on the theme of the evolution of feminist consciousness. The pieces complement each other in manifold ways, showing how mythic female revelations transform themselves into heroic feminist actions, and how the dreams and intuitions of the Mothers are transmitted to the Daughters through the ecstatic, compassionate cycling of female energy, which is the powerful force of womanlove alive in the universe today. It is Jovette Marchessault's unique visionary voice that endows the poetic word with a resonance that sings of spiritual resurrection, and promises joy and jubilation in a world infused by womanvision in the Promised Land of the Amerindian continent.

NOTES

1 Mary Daly, *Gyn/Ecology: The Metaethics of Radical Feminism* (Boston: Beacon Press, 1978), p. 9.

2 *Ibid.*, pp. 10-11.

3 Marija Gimbutas, *Goddesses and Gods of Old Europe, 6500-3500 B.C.: Myths and Cult Images* (Berkeley and Los Angeles: University of California Press, 1982).

4 Adrienne Rich, "The Meaning of Our Love for Women Is What We Have Constantly to Expand," in *On Lies, Secrets, and Silence: Selected Prose 1966-1978* (New York: W.W. Norton, 1979), pp. 229-30.

★ ★ ★

Gloria F. Orenstein is an Associate Professor of Comparative Literature and the Program for the Study of Women and Men in Society at the University of Southern California in Los Angeles. She was cofounder of the Woman's Salon for Literature in New York. Her writings on contemporary women writers and artists have been published widely in both feminist and academic journals. She is the author of The Theatre of the Marvelous: Surrealism and the Contemporary Stage.

BIBLIOGRAPHY

Barbara Godard

WORKS BY JOVETTE MARCHESSAULT

BOOKS

Comme une enfant de la terre I: Le crachat solaire. Montreal: Leméac, 1975. Prix France-Québec, 1976.

La Mère des herbes. Montreal: Quinze, 1980.

Tryptique lesbien. Montreal: Pleine Lune, 1980.

La Saga des poules mouillées. Montreal: Pleine Lune, 1980. *Saga of the Wet Hens.* Trans. Linda Gaboriau. Vancouver: Talonbooks, 1983.

La terre est trop courte, Violette Leduc. Montreal: Pleine Lune, 1982.

Lettre de Californie. Montreal: Editions Nouvelle Optique, 1982.

Alice & Gertrude, Natalie & Renée et ce cher Ernest. Montreal: Pleine Lune, 1984.

ARTICLES

"Faits d'Hiver." *La Nouvelle Barre du jour,* No. 68-69 (septembre 1978), pp. 129-33.

"Nous n'écrivons plus pour les fonds de tiroirs." *Châtelaine,* 20 (janvier 1979), pp. 48-49, 66-75.

"Les vaches de nuit." *La Nouvelle Barre du jour,* No. 75 (février 1979), pp. 83-92.

"Il m'est encore impossible de chanter, mais j'écris." *Jeu,* 16 (1980), pp. 207-10.

"Les faiseuses d'anges." *La Nouvelle Barre du jour,* No. 87 (février 1980), pp. 19-29.

"Les Monstresses." *La Nouvelle Barre du jour,* No. 102 (avril 1981), pp. 7-12.

"XXX." *Québec français,* No. 47 (octobre 1982), pp. 11-12.

"Alice et Gertrude et Natalie et Renée et ce cher Ernest." (Excerpt) *La Nouvelle Barre du jour,* 13, No. 3 (novembre 1983), pp. 19-34. "Alice and Gertrude and

Natalie and René and dear Ernest." Trans. Basil Kingstone. *Canadian Fiction Magazine,* No. 47 (1983), pp. 58-64.

PRODUCTIONS OF PLAYS

"Les Vaches de nuit": 5 March 1979, Théâtre du Nouveau Monde, Montreal; Théâtre Expérimental des Femmes, Montreal, November 1979. "Night Cows": Woman's Salon, New York, Fall 1979; A Space, Toronto, 1 December 1980; Women and Words, Vancouver, July 1983.

"La Saga des poules mouillées": Théâtre du Nouveau Monde, Montreal, 24 April 1981.

"Saga of the Wet Hens": Tarragon Theatre, Toronto, 18 February 1982.

"La Terre est trop courte, Violette Leduc": Théâtre Expérimental des Femmes, Montreal, 5 November 1981. "The Edge of the Earth is Too Near, Violette Leduc," trans. Suzanne de Lotbinière Harwood: Ubu Repertory Theatre, New York, 16 October 1984; Montreal, 20 January 1985; Toronto, March 1985.

"Alice et Gertrude et Natalie et Renée et ce cher Ernest": Atelier Continu, Montreal, 20 October 1984.

WORKS ON JOVETTE MARCHESSAULT

INTERVIEWS

Bell, Gay. "Where Nest the Wet Hens." Interview with Michelle Rossignol and Jovette Marchessault. *Broadside* (February 1982), pp. 12-13.

Smith, Donald. "Jovette Marchessault: de la femme tellurique à la démythification sociale." *Lettres québécoises,* 27 (automne 1982), pp. 53-58.

Stanton, Julie. "Pour Jovette Marchessault c'a été: 'Tu crées où tu crèves.'" *Châtelaine,* 22 (juin 1981), pp. 110-14, 116, 118, 120.

Théoret, France. "Interview avec Jovette Marchessault." *Spirale,* No. 20 (juin 1981), p. 18.

CATALOGUES OF EXHIBITIONS

Orenstein, Gloria. Catalogue for *Huit Montréalaises.* Soho 20, New York, January 1980.

CRITICISM

Articles

Couillard, Marie. "Symphonies féministes." In *Gynocritics/Gynocritiques: Feminist Approaches to Canadian and Quebec Women's Writing.* Ed. Barbara Godard. Downsview: ECW, 1985.

Orenstein, Gloria. "Jovette Marchessault ou la Quête exstatique de la nouvelle chamane féministe." *Bulletin de la société des professeurs français en Amérique,* 1 (Fall 1979), pp. 37-57.

————. "Jovette Marchessault: The Ecstatic Vision-Quest of the New Feminist Shaman." *Lady Unique Inclination of the Night* (Autumn 1980), pp. 42-53.

————. "Preface." *La Mère des herbes.* Montreal: Quinze, 1980, pp. 9-17.

————. "The Telluric Women of Jovette Marchessault." *Fireweed,* Nos. 5/6 (Winter 1979/80), pp. 164-65.

Book Reviews

Bourassa, André G. "Le Théâtre qu'on publie: Poules d'eau et vaches de nuit." *Lettres québécoises,* 23 (automne 1981), pp. 37-38.

————. "Le Théâtre qu'on publie: Quand les poètes deviennent personnages." *Lettres québécoises,* 26 (été 1982), pp. 45-47.

Constantin, Louise. Compte-rendu de *Tryptique lesbien. Des luttes et des rires des femmes,* IV, No. 5 (juin 1981), pp. 43-44.

Cossette, Gilles. "Le Roman II: *La Mère des herbes* de Jovette Marchessault." *Lettres québécoises,* 20 (hiver 1980-1981), pp. 18-20.

Dionne, André. Compte-rendu de *Tryptique lesbien. Livres et auteurs québécois 1980.* Quebec: Les Presses de l'Université Laval, 1981, pp. 51-52.

Dumont, Monique. "Une filiation d'écritures: *La Saga des poules mouillées.*" *Spirale,* No. 20 (juin 1981), p. 19.

E.[liette] R.[ioux]. Compte-rendu de *Comme une enfant de la terre* de Jovette Marchessault. *Les têtes de pioche,* No. 5 (septembre 1976), p. 8.

Forsyth, Louise H. "Women Reclaim their Culture in Quebec: A Saga of Night Cows and Wet Hens." *Spirale: A Woman's Art and Culture Quarterly,* 1, No. 2 (Autumn 1981), pp. 12-13; in French, pp. 13, 15.

L'Hérault, Pierre. Compte-rendu de *La Mère des herbes. Livres et auteurs québécois 1980.* Quebec: Les Presses de l'Université Laval, 1981, pp. 50-51.

Michaud, Ginette. Compte-rendu de *La Terre est trop courte, Violette Leduc. Jeu,* 24 (1982), pp. 124-25.

Orenstein, Gloria. "Plant Mother: Mythic Vision." Review of *La Mère des herbes. New Woman's Times: The Feminist Review,* 12 (October 1980).

Théoret, France. "Un livre impatient: Marchessault, *La Mère des herbes.*" *Spirale,* No. 10 (juin 1980), pp. 1, 4.

Yanacopoulo, Andrée. "Lettre de Montréal." Compte-rendu de *Lettre de Californie. Spirale,* No. 32 (mars 1983), p. 4.

Reviews of Plays

Corbeil, Carol. "Dream Comes True for Marchessault." *Globe and Mail,* 28 May 1981, p. 19.

―――. "Feminist Version of Quebec Writers." *Globe and Mail,* 30 May 1981, p. E5.

Dassylvia, Martial. "Jovette Marchessault: l'écriture à voix haute." *La Presse,* 25 avril 1979, pp. C1, C6.

Harris, Norma. "Magic of Wet Hens Misdirected." *Globe and Mail,* 20 February 1982, p. E9.

Marois, Thérèse. "Mythes féminins: *La Saga des poules mouillées* au TNM." *Jeu,* 20 (1981), pp. 52-56.

Radio and Television Criticism

Interviews with audience of *Saga of the Wet Hens,* Tarragon Theatre, CJRT, February 1982.

Orenstein, Gloria. "Jovette Marchessault au Salon des Femmes, New York." Radio-Canada, Montreal, fall 1979.

―――. "Le retour de la Déesse." With Françoise d'Eaubonne, Leonora Carrington and Jovette Marchessault. CBC French Network Television, Montreal, spring 1980.

OTHER RELEVANT WORKS

Godard, Barbara. "Bibliography of Feminist Criticism/Bibliographie de la critique féministe." *Gynocritics/Gynocritiques: Feminist Approaches to Canadian and Quebec Women's Writing.* Downsview: ECW, 1985.

―――. "Francophone Canada." In *Women Writers in Translation: An Annotated Bibliography 1945-1982.* Ed. Marjorie Resnick and Isabelle de Courtivron. New York: Garland, 1984, pp. 93-112.

Gould, Karen. "Setting Words Free: Feminist Writing in Quebec." *Signs,* 6, No. 4 (Summer 1981), pp. 617-42.

Gwyn, Sandra. "The Literary Arts." In *Women in the Arts in Canada,* vol. 7, Report of the Royal Commission on the Status of Women. Ottawa: Information Canada, 1971, pp. 60-98.

Makward, Christiane. "Quebec Women Writers." *Women and Literature,* 7, No. 1 (1979), pp. 3-11.

Yvonne M. Klein   *Jovette Marchessault*

JOVETTE MARCHESSAULT, the self-educated daughter of a working class family, was born in Montreal in 1938.

She is an accomplished sculptor, as well as a writer. In 1974 she began her first novel, *Comme une enfant de la terre* which won the Prix France-Quebec. Two novels followed, as well as several theatrical works including the celebrated *The Saga of the Wet Hens*.

Lesbian Triptych is her first full-length non-theatrical work to appear in English translation.

YVONNE M. KLEIN was born in New York City and came to Montreal, the home of her mother's family for generations, in 1969. She teaches English and women's literature at Dawson College and has been active in the Montreal feminist movement. She translated Renée Vivien's *The Woman of the Wolf* with Karla Jay in 1983 and is the author of numerous articles and book reviews.